# THE
# BLESSING

......................................................

## BRIAN KENT

Lincoln, Nebraska

Publisher's Note: This is a work of fiction. Names, characters, places, and incidents are a product of the author's imagination. Locales and public names are sometimes used for atmospheric purposes. Any resemblance to actual people, living or dead, or to businesses, companies, events, institutions, or locales is completely coincidental.

Book Layout ©2013 BookDesignTemplates.com

Ordering Information:
Quantity sales. Special discounts are available on quantity purchases by corporations, associations, and others. For details, contact the "Special Sales Department" at the address above.

The Blessing/ Brian Kent. -- 1st ed.

ISBN-13:978-1979602136

ISBN-10:1979602131

*Dedicated to the awake and blessed with understanding.*

# CHAPTER ONE

# A BREAK IN THE MONOTONY

Slamming his hand down on the snooze, Braden took cover from the incessant sunlight penetrating his room. He hadn't been back to work since the heart attack, but the need to maintain a routine gave him a sense of stability in a lifestyle which had been drastically changed. Thus, the daily struggle with the alarm became the one annoying consonant he could rely on.

Curled up in his comforter, his bare feet were not quite ready to meet the cold hardwood floor. His thoughts turned to another monotonous day. *Lunch at*

*Upstream sounds good. I should check out today's special.*

The doctors suggested a month of limited exercise and plenty of rest while the new prescriptions took effect. With his days consisting of short walks around the Old Market neighborhood, endless hours of television, and browsing the internet, his state of mind felt tested. As a result, Braden gained five pounds; and the lack of activity and adventure was becoming depressing.

Braden rolled out of bed, not allowing his morning adversary another chance to disturb his peaceful yet dull existence. He opened the kitchen cupboard and pulled out a box of instant oatmeal. *Damn it. Last packet. Got to go to the store today.*

Placing a bowl of water in the microwave, he watched it spin. The boiling beads rose to the top. *Huh. A watched pot does boil. God, I'm pathetic.* Making himself comfortable in the living room, he turned on the morning news, awaiting his oatmeal to cool. *Better make a grocery list. I don't want to forget anything.* He was in the process of jotting down a few items when his cell phone interrupted his train of thought. He didn't recognize the number. *It's got to be a bill collector or telemarketer.* He let it ring until something convinced him to answer.

He gave in. "Yeah."

"How you feeling today, Sunshine?" a woman asked.

"Fat! Who's this?"

"That's too bad. I wanted to talk to Braden," the female tease continued.

It's Connie, silly. Your nurse from Dempster Memorial. You gave me your business card, remember?"

"Very funny! May I ask who this is?"

Stunned by the unexpected phone call, Braden straightened up on the couch. "Oh, hi Connie! What a nice surprise."

"I normally don't check on former patients, but not everybody gives me a phone number, either. How are you doing?"

"I am bored as hell, but I feel fine. The daytime television and internet just doesn't cut it!"

"Well, let's do something about that. I'm on my way to Omaha today and was wondering what you were doing for lunch. Are you busy?"

"Not at all!"

"Have any suggestions on where to go?"

"What are you in the mood for?"

"Something light and maybe a drink or two."

"How about the Old Market Upstream?"

"Sure! Sounds great. So how are you feeling? Still taking your pain pills?"

"Nah, they made me woozy. I'm already a couch potato the way it is. I don't need to be a zombie, too."

"I kind of figured you'd need company. That's why I thought I'd come up."

"Well, that sounds fun. Shall we say, out front of Upstream around 11:00?"

"Looking forward to it. I'll see you then!"

It is not uncommon for a patient to develop a crush on their immediate care provider, and his attraction to Connie was no exception. In his brief three day stay, a connection between the two seemed inevitable. Braden hoped it wasn't a passing infatuation.

Braden hadn't been out with a woman in over a year, and his exuberance soon turned to anxiety. Almost burning his mouth, he hastily finished his bowl of oatmeal. *What do I wear?*

Shuffling through his closet, his favorite dress shirt was nowhere to be found. *When did I wear it last? Did Josh borrow it?* He looked in his office. He looked in the hall closet. *There's only one place it could be.* Tucked in a ball between the washer and dryer, he found it wadded up and wrinkled. *Damn it.* He gave it a smell. *This won't do.*

One of his Mother's quick fixes came to mind. Spraying the shirt with a water bottle and a spritz of cologne around the collar, he tossed it in the dryer.

Jumping in the shower, his first date jitters seemed to run down the drain with the cascade of hot water. His attention turned to an opening monologue. *Women make up their minds about a man within the first five minutes. I have to be witty and charming.* As the lines bounced around in his head, they sounded prefabricated and rehearsed. Convincing himself of their redundancy, he made the conscience decision to be himself. *She has already met me. She must like something about me. She wouldn't drive all the way up here if she didn't.* Feeling confident and refreshed, he rubbed his cheeks noting a two-day stubble. *This has to go.* Braden crawled out of the shower. The steamed up mirror gave no reflection. Giving the glass a quick swipe of his towel, the shock of an older man standing behind him caught him off guard.

Covering himself, he spun around. "What the fuck! Who are you?"

The old man did not utter a single word. Dark circles encompassed his eyes, conveying an empathetic stare on the verge of tears. His disheveled clothing was reminiscent of a transient who had wandered into the complex.

Braden was pissed. "Why are you in my apartment?"

The man continued his sad but silent mime routine.

"Do you speak English? What do you want?"

With no response, Braden lost his patience. He reached out to grab the old man's shoulder. His visitor faded right in front of him! Braden fell back against the bathroom sink with his mouth wide open!

"Are you fucking kidding me?"

Unhinged over the personal experience, Braden rubbed his eyes. *Am I hallucinating?* Reaching out where the man had stood. *He was right here! I saw his face!* Wasting no time and still in his towel, he marched into his office and pulled out a bottle of Holy Water from his briefcase. *That will be enough of this shit!* Wanting to put an immediate end to the possible haunting, he sprayed the divine liquid all over his domicile while reciting prayers and marking crucifixes on every doorway.

"Whoever you are, you are not wanted here! You have no right to be in my home!"

Rattled and shivering, Braden not only had to get ready but now he needed to calm down. His doctor's warning resonated in his ears, *"Once you have a heart attack, you are susceptible to having another."* This worried the 48-year-old, and shocks like this one were not welcome.

Grabbing his trusty bottle of Fireball out of the freezer, he kicked back in his recliner and took a couple of tugs. The alcohol's burn slid down his throat providing him a brief euphoric moment of tranquility. He closed his eyes and allowed his body to sink into the oversized chair. The breather and shot seemed to be working until his ears picked up the second hand ticking on the living room clock. *Shit! I have to be there in thirty minutes!*

A little hesitant to go back in the bathroom, he quickly shaved in the kitchen then got dressed. Just before he scurried out the door, he shouted out one last order. "You are not welcome here! Stay out!"

# CHAPTER TWO

# FIRST DATE

B raden arrived at the restaurant out of breath, yet five minutes early. Antsy, he realized he had never seen Connie without her nurse's uniform. Replaying their past interactions, he was hoping her blue eyes would be a giveaway. Pacing back and forth on the broken sidewalk, he lit up a smoke.

A woman's voice called out, "You know you shouldn't be smoking, right?"

Recognizing her voice, Braden dropped his cigarette about facing into a vision of beauty approaching from half a block away. As he watched her, time slowed to a crawl. He took in every detail of the moment. Her street clothes accented a curvaceous body, which, until now, Braden could only mentally visualize. Once she drew close enough, the eyes which stole his heart a month prior regained their hold causing Braden's insides to do cartwheels.

"Well, hello blue eyes. Ever been here before?"

"No, but it looks nice."

"Its one of my favorites. Would you like to eat inside or out?"

"Let's go inside," Connie replied gazing in the windows.

The two were seated at a cozy booth. Once they settled in, a waiter arrived to take their drink orders.

"Do you like beer?" Braden asked.

"Sure. A beer sounds good."

"They have a brewery right here in the building." He then turned to the waiter, "The lady and I will have a draw of the Capitol Pale Ale."

Once they were alone, Connie's concerns rose to the surface. "Still smoking and drinking I see."

"Yeah, but I've cut way back on both. I only had three smokes this morning."

"That's good. I don't want you in an ER again."

"Hey, is this a professional or social meeting?"

"You're right. Sometimes my inner nurse can't help herself." She grabbed Braden's hand from across the table.

Not knowing what to think of this unexpected sign of affection, his natural instincts took over giving her fingers a gentle squeeze. Connie grazed her thumb across his knuckles inserting her intentions with a look he was unable to deny. Normally in control of his emotions, Braden buckled under her advance somehow knowing the moment was real. Both were in uncharted territory, hopelessly lost without a care in the world or a hand on the wheel. Though their descent had hit its mark, Braden convinced himself to moderate the fall. "So, are you here to see me, or do you have some business to take care of?"

"To be quite honest, I have three days off and thought it would be nice to see you again."

He managed to maintain his cool exterior, "Wow, that's quite a drive. What time did you leave this morning?"

"About 7:00."

"Do you have a hotel room lined up?"

"I thought you might be able to help me with those accommodations. I don't know Omaha very well."

"When do you have to be back?"

"My shift starts Monday evening at 11:00."

"So we have the whole weekend?"

Her glance from across the table jettisoned every ounce of oxygen from his body. "Yes, I'd like to spend all three days with you."

The budding romance continued over glasses of Moscato until mid-afternoon. With the wine beginning to go to their heads, Braden suggested they go for a walk through the Old Market.

The couple made their way up and down the vintage sidewalks. A little hole in the wall specializing in holiday decorations caught Connie's eye. "What's your favorite holiday?"

"I'm partial to Halloween and Christmas. What about you?"

"I love Christmas. I love the lights and all the traditions. Can we go in here?"

BRIAN KENT

Connie dragged Braden into the crowded shop. After twenty minutes of perusing the narrow aisles of endless ornaments, Braden felt nature calling and excused himself. Upon returning, he found Connie waiting outside the novelty shop holding a small bag. Handing it to Braden, she whispered, "This is for you."

Reaching into the bag, he pulled out a ceramic ghost holding a heart. The token took Braden by surprise. An immediate rush of emotion came over him in the form of a broad grin. "Why, thank you. This is very thoughtful."

Drawing closer, she placed her hands around his, "It has a double meaning. Not only has my favorite ghost hunter captured my heart, but I want him to take care of his."

Caught up in her advances, the touching gesture annihilated his collective demeanor resulting in a passionate lip-lock. She pulled back just long enough to say, "I've been waiting almost a month for that."

Finishing their hand in hand tour of the Old Market, the consummate gentleman asked, "Where did you park? Can I walk you to your car?"

Fearing an end to such a beautiful day, Connie again led from the front, "Sure, but where am I staying?"

"There's a Hilton about three blocks from my complex. Does that sound good?"

"That's nice, but I'd rather stay with you."

Braden's logic and relationship prowess left him unable to pick up on her forward approach. *Is she short on cash?* Mother Nature gave him a nudge stepping in with the reply, "Absolutely!"

CHAPTER THREE

# INTERRUPTIONS

The couple arrived at the seven-story apartment complex Braden called home. Its turn of the century industrial appeal maintained its underived appearance. The necessary upgrades were hardly noticeable, offering the illusion of a well-constructed building which had outlasted all of its neighbors. Its charm took Connie by surprise. "Nice place! Have you lived here long?"

"About two years. Originally this was an old fixture plant and warehouse in the early 1900's. The rent is reasonable, it's secure, and the units are spacious."

Braden escorted Connie up the old renovated freight elevator to his fifth-floor residence. Her eyes widened as she was led through the door to an expansive wide open flat. Its massive windows looked out over the Omaha skyline inviting the city's lights to bounce off the twelve-foot ceilings. "Very impressive!"

Picking up his socks and putting dirty dishes in the sink he sheepishly said, "Sorry, I wasn't expecting company. I left in a hurry this morning."

"Oh stop it. It's beautiful! What a view!"

"Yeah, I like it. I was one of the first tenants."

"Who did your interior decorating?"

"I did. I found this living room set at an estate sale. The rest I just pieced together."

"Well, you have a good eye. Very tasteful."

"Thanks. Hey, its close to dinner time. Do you like Italian?"

"Sure. What did you have in mind?"

"Caniglia's delivers. We could eat here and catch a movie on Netflix."

"That sounds great."

"Cool. Take your shoes off and make yourself at home."

Braden called in the order while Connie explored the rest of the apartment. Wandering into Braden's office, she noticed ten numbered metal cases on the floor. One was open containing Holy Water and scripted prayers. Curious, she began reading the sacred petitions. The words gave her an uneasy feeling. *What does he get himself into? Is he dealing with demons?* She gently laid the prayers back in the case. Scanning his desk, she found a book with his name on the front cover. *Hmmm. He's written a book. Looks creepy though.*

"Actually, I've written three books on the paranormal," Braden stated standing in the office entryway.

Connie spun around red-faced grabbing her chest. "My Lord, you about gave me a heart attack!"

"I'm sorry. I'll stomp down the hallway next time." He gave her a wink and a smirk.

"So, how long have you been doing this ghost hunting?"

"Almost a decade now."

"While we are on the subject, what was wrong with that house in Dempster?"

"A tragic past which built up into a negative energy that refused to leave. I just got a call from the lady who lives there. She said the house has been quiet ever since we left."

Connie remembered something Josh told her at the hospital. "Your brother mentioned something happened while you flat lined. What was that about?"

The conversation was interrupted by a knock at the door. He gave her a 'just a moment gesture,' as he paused to come up with an answer.

Braden peeked through the peephole seeing no one through the fisheye. Engaging the security chain, he opened the door. "Hello?" With no response, he removed the chain, popping his head into the hallway. No one was in sight. *Huh...I know I heard a knock.*

"You did hear a knock, didn't you?"

"Yes. Three knocks."

"Whoever it was didn't give me a chance. There was no one there."

"Maybe it was one of your ghosts. Do you make house calls?" Connie giggled.

Connie's comment reminded Braden of the morning episode, leaving him unresponsive with a concerned look on his face. *I didn't mention anything before, did I? Should I warn her? Should I bring up this morning's occurrence?*

"I was just kidding, Braden. What's wrong?"

"Oh, its nothing really."

"No, tell me. Is it something I said?"

Deep in thought, he left her hanging. *What would she think if I told her? Would she think I'm nuts?*

"For the love of Pete, Braden, tell me what's wrong."

*If we hit it off, she needs to know. Especially if she's staying the night.* "It's funny you brought that up. Before I left this morning, I had an experience in the bathroom."

"Meaning?"

"I was getting ready to shave, and an apparition of an old man appeared behind me."

"You're not teasing me, are you?"

"No. Unfortunately, I am not."

Connie pointed at the floor, "There was an actual ghost....in this apartment....today?"

"As sure as I am standing here."

"No one broke into your apartment? You weren't hallucinating off of pain pills and booze?"

"Neither. I think I would know what an apparition would look like. He was tall, fairly old, distressed didn't say a word. Part of him was vaporous before he dissipated."

"Do you know who he is? Did he follow you home?"

"Are you saying you believe?"

"Being around death, I have experienced some things I can't explain. I guess you could say I am open-minded about it."

"Well then, let's get comfortable in the living room. This may take a while."

Braden started from the beginning, explaining the horrific experiences he had as a child.

"Are you sure these experiences were not a figment of your youthful imagination?"

"I wondered the same thing. This is why we did the investigation a month ago. If you would've been there, you would have understood. The evidence was overwhelming."

Connie didn't know what to think. "I'd like to see and hear this evidence."

"I'll be right back." Braden strolled down the hallway to his office when there was another knock at the door. "Can you get that? It must be our dinner!"

Connie peeked through the peephole. No delivery man. She unlocked the door and pulled it open. Nothing but a silent empty hallway. *What the hell!*

Braden strutted back into the living room with laptop in hand. "What's the grand total?"

With no reply, Braden looked up from his laptop. "What's wrong? Where's dinner?"

"It just happened again! You heard someone knocking, right?"

"You're kidding?"

BRIAN KENT

"Not at all." Connie was visibly shaken. "Is it safe for me to be here?"

Placing his laptop down, Braden glanced up and down the hall straining his ear for any sign of movement. "It was just knocking...just noise. Maybe its the neighbors hanging a picture on the wall."

"No. I distinctly heard knocking on your door!"

"Could be kids playing a prank. Two teenagers live three doors down."

Trying to wrap her mind around Braden's logic, she reluctantly let her guard down. With a loving embrace, Braden could feel the earthquake of fear jetting through her gradually subsiding in his arms. There was a serenity in his inclusion, a confident and collective calm, transferring from one to the other. Neither wanted to let go when the door buzzer rang.

"What the fuck!" Braden pulled away to answer. "Yes?"

"Caniglias! Is this Braden Cabrera?"

"Yeah...Come on up to 501."

Braden turned to Connie. "Looks like we need to take time out."

Connie couldn't help herself, "At least there was someone at the door this time!"

# CHAPTER FOUR

# ARE GHOSTS ALWAYS AROUND?

The couple finished their candlelit dinner, grabbed their wine glasses, and made themselves comfortable on the couch. Braden programmed the remote for Netflix fidgeting through the numerous categories, and unaware Connie's mind was elsewhere. *Am I safe here? Does this guy have ghosts living with him? Are they watching us right now?*

"Comedy? Chick flick? Action? What sounds good?"

Connie stared out at the Omaha skyline. Their previous discussion was taking precedence. Oblivious to his movie proposals, "Are ghosts always around?"

Braden chose his response carefully. "Is that what's bothering you? What do you think?"

"We can't see them! There is no way to know! One could be sitting here right now, and we wouldn't know it."

"Yes. I guess that could be a possibility. Have you ever lost a loved one? Someone close to you?"

She lowered her head, "My dad passed away five years ago."

"Your father could be keeping an eye on you. Is that such a bad thing?"

"No, I guess not."

"Have you ever been harmed by something you couldn't explain?"

"No. But I was frightened once! Some paperwork unexpectedly fell on the floor at the med center."

"Were you hurt?"

"No."

"Did you try to rationalize the situation? Where did the paperwork fall from?"

"Well, no. That paperwork was on top of that file cabinet for months. It didn't make sense for it to fall off."

Braden's inner investigator made its appearance, "Did anyone have a window open? Did someone bump the file cabinet? Was the paperwork under an air vent? Did someone recently add more paperwork to the stack?"

"Hey! If you believe ghosts are real, why are you questioning me?"

"If we don't question all possibilities, then we may never get to the truth. The people we try to help rely on our neutral honesty. We want to find the real thing. Keeping that in mind, it is important to rule out logical explanations first. Right?"

*The Blessing*

"Since you put it that way, yes."

"Now do you want to talk about this all night, or do you want to watch a movie?"

"I'm getting a little freaked out. Let's watch a comedy."

"Fair enough."

The couple cuddled on the couch, periodically breaking out in laughter at the antics of Chris Farley. Halfway through the movie, Connie excused herself to use the restroom. Braden paused the flick and refilled their wine glasses. "We're about out of wine." There was no response.

A few minutes had passed when Connie's extended bathroom visit drew his attention. *Is she okay in there? Is she snooping through the medicine cabinet?*

"Con? You okay?"

The sound of the door opening convinced Braden to turn and look. Connie emerged from the lavatory in a sheer floor-length negligee. The hall light behind her silhouetted stunning curves hiding beneath the near see-through gown. Gently placing both glasses on the coffee table, Braden surrendered to her advance meeting her halfway in a hypnotic trance. No words were exchanged as they converged in a lustful kiss. Like a lioness with her prey, the temptress led Braden to the master bedroom.

The lovemaking became ravenous as their hands and lips took turns exploring each other's body. Their entwined sweat soaked bodies moved in a rhythmic syncopation as if each knew exactly what the other needed. The desired result was reached in an explosion of spasmodic ecstasy causing both to collapse in exhaustion. With their hunger satisfied, they fell asleep in each other's arms.

Around two in the morning, sirens yanked Braden out of dreamland. Rubbing his eyes, he slowly pulled back the covers careful not to awaken his lover. Flashing red and blue lights illuminated Farnam Street. A police cruiser and ambulance were attending to an older gentleman lying on the sidewalk. *This is becoming a nightly occurrence.*

Connie was still fast asleep. The full moon's illuminant glow shined through the window accenting her every feature. *She is so pretty. I'm a lucky man.* Pulling the comforter over her shoulders, he gave her a peck on the cheek.

Turning to go to the bathroom, Braden gasped. Like a peeping Tom, the old man had returned standing at the foot of his bed.

"Not you again!" Braden whispered.

The apparition stood still as the night with tears running down his sunken cheeks. His facial expression resonated a depression telepathically communicating his deep-seated pain. The spirit reached out for help with both hands. The old man's gesture overwhelmed Braden with despair.

"I don't know how to help you," Braden softly iterated out loud.

*The Blessing*

Now awake, Connie rolled over. "Who are you talking to?"

"Don't freak out, but the old man is here. Again!"

Connie sat up in bed looking around the room. "Where? I don't see anyone."

Braden pointed to the foot of the bed. "He's standing right here!"

Accommodating his assertion, she got out of bed giving the space a once-over. "There is no one here, babe! Are you okay?"

"You don't see this guy standing here?"

"No, I don't. I think you are sleepwalking. Come back to bed."

Puzzled by the lack of confirmation, Braden leaned towards the elderly gentleman. "You're not wanted here."

Now curled back up in the comforter, Connie overheard the one-sided conversation. "Hey, if you want me to leave, I will!"

"No, no, not you. Him!"

"There is no one there, Braden. Come back to bed."

Unnerved over the circumstance, Braden questioned his sanity. *Am I seeing things? Is this an illusion?* Cautiously approaching the elder, he whispered in the old man's ear, "You're not real. Go away." With that, the old man faded away taking his disconsolate burden with him.

Once back in bed, Connie snuggled her warm body against his. "Let's talk about this tomorrow."

# BRIAN KENT

CHAPTER FIVE

# THE BUILDING WITH A HISTORY

C onnie awoke at 6:00 a.m. Not ready to be seen in smudged makeup and bed hair, she jumped in the shower and put on a fresh face. All cleaned up and still beaming from the previous day, she made her way to the kitchen. Planning a surprise breakfast in bed, she opened the fridge stunned by a few bottles of Michelob Ultra, a tub of butter, and a head of shriveled lettuce. She advanced her search to the barely stocked cupboards. *What does this guy eat for breakfast?*

"Oatmeal. The doctor wants me to eat oatmeal. But I'm out," boomed his voice from the bedroom.

"How did you know what I was thinking?"

"I heard the fridge open and close."

Connie wandered back to the bedroom. "Well, I'm hungry. Is there a store close by?"

With his head under the covers, Braden mumbled, "What are you doing up at this ungodly hour?"

With her hands on her hips, she responded, "So I see you aren't a morning person."

"I am! But I haven't heard an alarm go off yet."

Pulling down the comforter, he noticed Connie dressed and ready for the day. "Wow, there is nothing coyote ugly about you!"

Connie jumped on him as a tickle war ensued. In the heat of the wrestling match, she uttered, "Oh yeah. Well, at least I don't sleepwalk while talking to imaginary men at two o'clock in the morning."

His assault on her ribs came to an abrupt halt. The smile left Braden's face leading Connie to believe she had struck a nerve. Without a word, Braden got out of bed and went to the bathroom shutting the door behind him. Connie approached the door. "Hey, look. I'm sorry. I was just teasing."

"Can a man have some privacy while he uses the restroom?"

"Ain't nothing I haven't seen before!" Connie leaned against the wall. *He certainly is over sensitive about this ghost thing. Maybe it's best to drop it.*

Still in his pajama bottoms, Braden exited the bathroom marching down to his office. Laying low for the moment, Connie tiptoed down the hall just as Braden placed a call. "Hey, you busy today?"

Wondering who he was talking to, she edged closer to the door. The one-sided conversation peeked her interest. "I think something has followed me home. I've witnessed two full-bodied appearances within a twenty-four hour period. Same guy both times."

Braden continued his report. "No, I don't know it is. But I have company. Connie from Dempster stopped by."

Connie overheard her name, and stood in the office doorway listening. "No, I haven't called Caleigh. Her and Rudy are still out of town." He concluded his call. "I'll see you around noon."

With her arms crossed she asked, "So who's stopping by?"

"Brother Josh is coming over for lunch. He's looking forward to seeing you again, and we are going to do a little snooping around."

"Snooping for what?"

"You, my dear, are going to witness your first paranormal investigation."

"Do you mean what I think you mean?"

"Yep. Something is in this building, and its time to get to the bottom of it."

"I don't want to be here for that!"

"It's not what you think. You will be fine. Nothing will happen."

"Are you positive?"

"Cross my heart and hope to..."

Connie cut him off mid-sentence. "Don't you EVER say that again!"

Braden's cell phone interrupted. "Hello?... Hey, Elsa, what's up?"

Connie's mind raced with all sorts of ghost hunting horrors. *My Lord, his whole team is going to be here. We're going to spend the entire afternoon talking to ghosts. It's going to be dark, and I don't care how comfortable he is around that, something is going to jump out and touch me. I just know it!*

Braden cupped his hand over the phone's mouthpiece. "Connie! Nothing is going to happen to you. Please calm down." Returning to his conversation with Elsa, "Yes, the address is 945 Farnam St. Its the old Omaha Fixture facility."

Braden finished his call. "Elsa is going to do some research on the building. She'll either call or stop by later."

"So how many are coming by?"

"Looks like Josh, Daris, and possibly Elsa."

Connie's inner Mother took charge, "Why don't you get cleaned up? Then we can run down to the store. We'll need some groceries for lunch."

Braden immediately headed for the shower. "Yes, ma'am!"

The couple returned from the store, weighed down with ten bags of groceries. "Now you know why my fridge is so empty. It took us forever to load all of this in the elevator."

"Well, now you're stocked up for a week or two. Not to mention, you now have fruits and vegetables instead of frozen pizza and Ramen noodles."

"But I like Tombstone pizza!"

"And so do I, Sweetheart, but within reason. Not twice a week!"

The debate over healthy living was interrupted by a phone call from Elsa. Having completed her historical research, she had much to report. "There have been three deaths on or close to the property. A young boy was hit by a car and killed on Farnam Street. Looks like it happened right outside of your building. But this doesn't match your description. We have a woman who died in a work-related accident while it was Omaha Fixture. It happened in 1945. She was only 24 at the time. She may have been working there during the war effort. Blunt force trauma to the skull."

"My God," Braden broke in. "What could have caused that?"

"It doesn't say, but her death was apparently instant. However, our last culprit may be your man. Charles L. Camfield died in an elevator accident in 1958. One of the cables allegedly broke, and the car free-fell five stories while he was in it. The story made the front page of the Omaha Bee newspaper. He was 62 years old. The coroner believed he died of a massive heart attack coupled with extensive injuries. Now get this, Charles was one of the chief mechanics at Omaha Fixture. Guess where maintenance was located in the plant?"

"Fifth floor?"

"You got it! By the way, is your friend African-American?"

"I don't know, its hard to tell. All I can make out is male features."

"Well, that's it. Three deaths and none of them were natural. Do you want me to look further into Charles' background?"

"Yeah, that would probably be a good idea if you don't mind."

"I don't mind. I'm just as bored as you are. By the way, when are you going to be ready to start up again?"

"Shouldn't be too long. I see the doctor in two weeks. I'll let you know."

"Sounds good. Hope you're feeling better. I'll keep you posted on what I find."

Connie was busy putting groceries away and rummaging through Braden's shelves. "One thing about empty cupboards...they are easy to organize. What did Elsa find out?"

"She may have discovered something. At least we have a lead to go on."

"Well, that's good. I'm making BLT's for everyone. Okay?"

"Awesome! They should be here any minute."

CHAPTER SIX

BEHIND THE WALL

Ecstatic to be doing their first case in a month, Josh and Daris arrived a little early. Braden's fist bumps and the smell of frying bacon greeted them at the front door. "Wow, you can sure tell there's a woman in the house. Where's my sandwich?" Josh spouted with a smirk on his face. Connie rolled her eyes, flipping the sizzling strips. He added, "It's nice to see you again, Connie."

Gathered at the dining room table, the conversation turned to the business at hand. "Who would ever think we'd be investigating your place?" Josh started, "Do you think you brought something home?"

"At first, I considered that. But then I got a report from Elsa. I never thought of researching this building before I moved in. Within an hour, Elsa discovered three unnatural deaths on the property. One could be our target."

The situation reminded Daris of an investigator's number one rule. "I thought you always told us; we shouldn't investigate our own homes. Doesn't this go against protocol?"

"That's why you are here, my friend. You and Josh are going to investigate. You are to treat me like a client. I am on the sidelines today."

"Well, that's going to be a little strange. You always run things."

"You and Josh both know what to do. I'll fill both of you in on Elsa's report. Then you may start with the sweep, okay?"

Connie brought in three plates filled with BLT's and fresh veggies. "Nobody should ghost hunt on an empty stomach. Now dig in."

"Hey, I like her Braden. She's a keeper," Josh chimed in with a smart-ass grin.

After lunch, the teammates pulled out the mysterious cases in Braden's office. Cameras and equipment Connie had never seen before were laid out on the dining room table. "So this is what was in the cases. What does all of this stuff do exactly?"

Braden pointed out each piece, "Primarily it's used for detection. We'll be setting up surveillance cameras in case our friend wants to make an appearance. Daris will be taking environmental readings all afternoon. We believe entities are capable of causing minor changes in their general proximity."

She gave Braden a skeptical yet puzzled look. "Like what?"

"Such as temperature. You know, cold spots. The device he's holding now takes barometric and thermal readings. Daris will also be checking electromagnetic fields and low sound frequencies."

"Interesting. So has this type of study ever produced results?"

"Many times. The case in Dempster alone provided numerous extreme changes. One cold spot produced a ten-degree temperature drop."

"So how did you know it wasn't caused by an open window or air vent?"

"You are one smart woman. You may end up being an investigator yet!" He wrapped his arm around her waist. "We do our best to control the investigation's environment. All windows are closed, and HVAC units are shut down. Then Daris does what we call a sweep. During the sweep, Daris takes base readings in each room. This way we know what readings are standard for the area."

"All of this sounds intriguing. Where are we going to be when all of this starts?"

"You and I will be watching everything on surveillance in my office while those two take care of business. Okay?"

"All right. I have to admit, it's a little overwhelming; but you have my curiosity up now."

Connie watched with intent as Daris and Josh meandered through each room of the condo. From time to time, one of the devices would light up, or let out a squelch. She'd ask Braden, "What was that?"

Braden snickered, "Its nothing, dear."

The sweep continued for a half an hour when Daris emerged from the master bedroom. "Hey B? Any idea what is behind the wall between your closet and bathroom door?"

"I have no idea. Why?"

"The Mel-Meter gave me a 135.5 milligauss reading from that wall. Something is cooking in there."

"Really! Let's go take a look!"

Both men marched down to Braden's bedroom. Daris was able to reenact the detection as the digital numbers rose over 100 milligauss. "This doesn't make sense, B. Even if all the wiring to this building ran through this one wall, the readings still wouldn't be this high. Not the way its shielded."

Braden tipped his head to one side. "Is the Mel working properly?"

Daris removed the meter from the wall. The display simultaneously dropped to 0.0. "Yep. She's working fine."

"Let me get a hold of Mr. Callahan. He should know."

Braden placed a call to the building's supervisor, leaving Daris running his meter up and down the wall. Connie was curious. "Does this mean a ghost is in there?"

Not taking his eye off the scanner, Daris answered, "I wouldn't say that, but something is definitely giving off a strong electromagnetic field."

## The Blessing

Mr. Callahan and his trusty toolbox arrived a few minutes later. The sometimes cranky old man was led into Braden's bedroom. "Okay, what's this all about?"

"We were wondering, Bob, if you knew what was behind this wall," Braden asked, aware of the superintendent's callous disposition.

"Why? Is something leaking?" the old man asked with a scowl on his face.

"Well...kinda. There are extremely high EM readings coming from it."

"Is this more of your ghost busting crap? I don't have time for this. I have a baseball game on!" Bob spouted, picking up his toolbox to leave.

"All I want to know is what's behind this wall," Braden pleaded to the old man who was attempting to exit.

With his back turned, he began marching down the hall, "An old utility room! Don't worry about it!"

Braden ran after him preventing his departure. "What do mean by old utility room?"

The agitated old cuss stared back at Braden, "A large generator and panel board. Nothing for you to worry about. None of it is hooked up. Now leave me alone!"

Struggling for answers, Braden continued with the antsy maintenance man, "Do you know what it was used for?"

"Look, young man, I've had about enough!"

"Please, Mr. Callahan. What was it used for?"

Figuring he wasn't going anywhere unless he answered, "It is old elevator equipment mounted in the wall. The contractors left it behind when they did the renovation. Are you happy now?"

Braden slowly let loose his grip on the old man's arm. Mr. Callahan stormed out of the condo, slamming the door behind him. Braden added things up. *Mr. Camfield worked on this floor. He died in an elevator.*

Daris interrupted his train of thought. "Um, Braden? The wall is no longer emitting a reading."

CHAPTER SEVEN

# NOT AGAIN

"You look like you just saw a ghost." Josh laughed. "What's up?"

"I think we may be onto something."

"I'm sure Connie is relieved to hear that! Okay, let's hear it."

Braden reported Elsa's findings, which caught Connie off guard. "So a man actually died in an elevator accident on this property?"

"I'm afraid so, Sweetie."

"People can die anywhere, Connie. You should know that," Josh added.

"I understand. The coincidences are just a little disturbing."

Braden gave her hand a reassuring squeeze. "Now you know why we do the research, Babe."

Braden, Josh, and Daris quickly set up surveillance for the afternoon's investigation. Once everything was in place, Josh and Daris began the EVP session in the master bedroom near the wall which enclosed the rumored utility room.

Josh made the introductions. "Good afternoon. My name is Josh Cabrera, and this is my friend, Daris Maxwell. My brother, Braden, lives in this apartment. He has asked us here to talk with you. May we know your name?"

Leaving a few seconds in between each question, Daris asked, "It has been brought to our attention... a man who used to work here... passed away in this general area. Am I speaking with Mr. Camfield?"

Another brief delay in the interrogation was followed by, "You've been seen twice. Is there something you want or need?"

Out of nowhere, one of the meters leaning up against the enclosing wall indicated a change in the electromagnetic field. Josh noted the reading verbally. "We have a blip on the KII meter. Is that you, Sir?" Trying to encourage the interaction, "This equipment will not harm you. It only lets us know of your presence. Are you with us now?"

In Braden's office, Connie was beside herself. "I don't know if I can do this. Is there a ghost in there with them?"

"They are only trying to communicate, Sweetie. We've done this hundreds of times. They're fine. No one will be hurt."

"Oh really? What about your ordeal in Dempster?"

"That was a heart attack, not a ghost."

Josh and Daris concluded their EVP session, bringing the voice recorder into the office for review. Daris hooked up the device to the office studio and hit play. To their astonishment, the first question reaped a reply introducing itself with a long drawn out, "Chaaaaazzz."

"Are you kidding me! What the hell is a Chaz?" Josh ranted.

"Chaz is short for Charles!" Braden inserted. "That's probably the name he went by."

Perplexed by the teammate's enthusiasm and candor, Connie had to say something. "Are you telling me that's a ghost talking right there, and you're not freaked out?"

"More like intrigued," Josh answered. "Let's hear the rest of it."

All four listened to the recording patiently awaiting another reply. Question after question went by without one single response, until it was asked, "Who do you want to talk to?" Immediately a male voice whispered two syllables.

"There is something there," Daris announced. "The first part has an 'A' in it."

"And I'm hearing an 'N' in the last part," Josh added.

"Hmmmm...A...N," Braden surmised. "Take that hissing out of it and give it some clarity, Daris."

Daris made some suitable adjustments. "Here. Try this."

The playback was very faint. Everyone bent their ear straining to understand the response. "I hear the 'A,'" Braden reported.

"And I hear the 'N'! Did it just say your name?" Connie asked in horror.

"I'm not sure. Could be."

"I don't think we should be doing this. Something doesn't feel right."

Not empathizing Connie's concern, Josh's spouted, "It's not like Braden can call an exterminator!"

Braden stepped in. "Now Josh. She's never seen or heard this stuff before. Give her a break." Turning to Connie, he said, "Sweetheart, we believe if we can just communicate with an entity, we may be able to discover their intent. What they want...Why their here. They may be reaching out..."

Suddenly, Braden grabbed his chest in dire agony. His disoriented glare broadened his eyes in disbelief. Bending over in pain, he let out an exasperated grunt. Connie yelled out, "Jesus Christ, not again! Somebody call 911!"

Josh jumped into action, almost dropping his phone in the process. His face went pale white as he watched his brother struggle to breathe. Each attempt seemed to stab Braden in the sternum contracting similar sympathy pain in his own chest. Having to leave the room, Josh impatiently continued his call in the hallway. When the emergency operator didn't answer right away, he started swearing. "Come on, dammit! Answer the fucking phone!"

Connie laid Braden down on the floor. "Don't you do this to me, Braden!"

## The Blessing

Braden's body went limp. Connie immediately started CPR and chest compressions. Her hands pushed down on his chest, and she cried out, "Dammit, Braden... wake up! Come back to me!"

Braden suddenly gasped for air, coughing and gagging. As he tried to sit up, Connie gently held him down. "Thank God," she sighed. "Please lie still. I think you may have had another heart attack. An ambulance is on the way."

Concerned for his friend, Daris added, "I thought we might have lost you for a minute. Good thing Connie was here. How do you feel?"

With heavy sweat running down his red cheeks, Braden took a couple of deep breaths uttering, "Lightheaded. For a minute there, I felt like I was falling. Then everything went blank."

"Well, you're back now, Hun," Connie kissed his forehead. "You're heading to the hospital."

# BRIAN KENT

CHAPTER EIGHT

# THE DIAGNOSIS

The doctor wandered into Braden's room finding Josh, Daris, and Connie surrounding his bed. "How are we doing, Mr. Cabrera?"

"I'd be better if I didn't have all of these wires hooked up to me."

The doctor reviewed the video monitor and scrolled back to see earlier feed before he responded, "Well then, let's take them off."

Connie's medical training made an appearance. "Shouldn't he be on twenty-four observation?"

"Normally, yes. But that's for people who have had a heart attack. Mr. Cabrera did not have a heart attack."

Unable to contain herself, Connie went off. "I'm a nurse, and I've witnessed many heart attacks. I know the signs. If Braden didn't go into cardiac arrhythmia, what the hell happened?"

"All of his readings come back normal. There is no sign of stress and the prescriptions he has been taking seem to be working." Turning to his patient,

"Did you have pain in your left arm, before the attack?"

"No. No pain at all."

"Where did the pain start?"

Pointing to his breastplate, Braden answered, "Right in here."

"Have you ever had esophageal unrest?"

"Speak English, Doc."

"Have you ever had extreme heartburn?"

"No."

Connie stepped in, "Are you insinuating his attack was caused by acid reflux?"

"More than likely," the doctor replied as he jotted down information on a pad. "I've seen this numerous times. The symptoms can be very similar."

Handing Braden a slip of paper, he added, "This is a prescription to ease stomach acid. It won't be counterproductive to your other medication. Give it a day or two to take full effect. Do you have any other questions?"

"As a matter of fact, I do. How can stomach acid cause a person to pass out? According to everyone, I was unconscious for a few minutes."

"Were you having trouble breathing?"

"Yes. There was extreme pain every time I tried to inhale."

"That's why you passed out. The pain kept you from inhaling normally. You weren't getting enough oxygen to your brain."

"Well, I guess that makes sense."

"I'll sign your release. If you have any more episodes, get in touch with my staff at this number. Have a good day, Mr. Cabrera."

Once the doctor left the room, Connie's skepticism showed. "I don't understand." Turning to Braden who was already pulling off monitor tabs, Connie continued on her rant. "Usually a patient shows signs of stomach issues, ulcers, or a hiatal hernia before it gets to this stage. Have you ever had bouts with heartburn before?"

Finally free of the EKG monitor, he answered, "No. Not that I can remember."

A member of the hospital staff wandered in. "Well, I see you've already removed your electrodes. You are free to go, Mr. Cabrera."

Back in the car, Connie was befuddled. "I have been a nurse almost twenty years. In those twenty years, I have witnessed hundreds of heart attacks. I have never seen anyone pass out from a severe case of acid reflux. I don't like this diagnosis."

"What else can I do, Con? The EKG's came back normal, and a well-respected member of the medical community disagrees with you."

"Get a second opinion."

"Look, this tummy ache has already cost me thousands of dollars. If the doctor wants me to take anti-acid medication, that's what I am going to do."

"What if he is wrong. That would mean you've had two heart attacks within thirty days. Your body could be trying to tell you something!"

"Right now, my body is telling me to go home and take a nap. I have had enough excitement for one day."

Realizing her warning was not being taken seriously, Connie stared out the window. Braden picked up on the silent treatment. "Are you going to pout all the way back home?"

"Why are men afraid to see a doctor? Does it attack your sense of mortality?"

"I just saw a doctor. It has nothing to do with fear. I don't want to waste money on a second opinion. And if you must know, I'm not afraid of dying."

"Well, I am, Braden! I have seen people die. Pass away right in front of me. It's not always peaceful."

"For God's sake, Connie! I'm not going anywhere! I have acid reflux...not cancer!"

"Doctors have been wrong before."

"So, this is about you. You're mad because your initial prognosis was incorrect."

"No. I just wanted the doctor to be a little more thorough."

"And that would have cost me thousands more."

"Wouldn't it be worth it? To be sure? For all we know, you may have a blocked passage or a valve malfunction."

"Sounds to me, like you'd want them to do open heart surgery."

"Don't be an ass. The doctor wasn't there when the attack occurred. I know what I saw, and I know the attack was not brought on by acid reflux. Apparently, my opinion means nothing."

Connie's sulk worried him. *Is she pissed because she's wrong or that I agreed with the doctor? Is this about her, or does she have a legitimate concern? How do I get out of this? I know...* "I respect your opinion, Con. But doctors go to school almost a decade so that they can properly diagnose and treat their patients. My medical care is relying on that education. So for now, I am going to follow the doctor's orders."

The rest of the ride back to Braden's condo was quiet. The increased tension between the two reached its high point when they approached Braden's door. Once Braden let them inside, Connie stormed down to the master bedroom. Grabbing her suitcase, she popped both latches and threw her unpacked clothing in its general direction. She stomped into the bathroom collecting her cosmetics and hairdryer. Braden was confused and heartbroken. "I take it you're leaving?"

"I have better things to do than worry about someone I just met. And by the way, I have an education in medicine, too!"

"Look, Connie, I just paid over two thousand dollars for tests and spent half an afternoon at Omaha General. I'm pretty sure they would know if I had a heart attack!"

"Fine! I'm glad you're okay. I'm heading back to Dempster!"

"Now, don't do this! It's eight o'clock at night! You won't get back home until after midnight!"

"Don't worry about me. I'm a big girl. I can handle myself!"

"Please stay until morning! I'll sleep on the couch."

Connie grabbed her purse and keys off the counter. With luggage in hand, she marched towards the door. Yanking it open, she uttered one last ultimatum, "Don't call. I won't answer." She slammed the door behind her.

Braden was hurting. *My God, what have I done? Was it something I said? Am I wrong here? Just when things were going so right, this happens.* Slumping in his recliner, his memories from the previous afternoon came rushing back. Feelings he hadn't felt in years surfaced in his throat. With a hard swallow, he re-engaged his tough exterior. "I need a drink."

## CHAPTER NINE

# SKID MARKS

Connie had been crying for miles. Her emotional state deterred her attention from the road, which caused her to periodically stray over the bumpy lane warnings. With thoughts of their romantic day fresh in her mind, she continued to relive each precious moment. She questioned her decision to leave numerous times, almost forcing herself to do an about-face. But she was determined to make a point. *All I asked for was a second opinion. I'm a registered nurse, for God's sake. I know I'm right.* Disdainful thoughts eased her pain, sidelining her heartache. Reaching into her purse, she grabbed a tissue and blew her nose. *If he doesn't understand my concerns or consider my opinion, he doesn't deserve me.*

Back and forth, she struggled between pride and her feelings. Eventually, her ire pointed towards the doctor and medical staff. *Its that doctor's incompetence. He's the problem. Braden is just following his orders.* Connie sported a smug grin. *I'll let Braden stew on this for a while. Serves him right for blowing me off. I got this. I'll give him a week or so to think about it. Then maybe I'll call.*

With only fifteen miles to go, the long day and drive began to take its toll. Connie fought to stay awake by opening the window and cranking up AC/DC in the disc player. Shaking her head, she refocused her eyes on the monotonous white lines buzzing down the centerline of the highway. It wasn't long before the thunderous music synched with the passing lines lulling her into a hypnotic trance. Catching herself nodding off again, she stuck her head out the window and allowed the cool summer breeze to revive her.

That's when she saw the two hundred pound buck standing in the middle of the road. Connie stepped on the brakes with both feet causing the tires to leave screeching skid marks down the asphalt surface. The car swayed to and fro until it corrected itself just in time to slam into the deer's side. The carcass slid up the hood of her Mustang smashing the windshield and spraying glass throughout the car's inner cavity. When the vehicle came to a complete stop, Connie was covered in glass and blood.

Once her bearings had returned, she surveyed the situation the best she could. *Okay...I'm alive and conscious. I just hit a deer. Am I okay?* She discovered the airbag had gone off. A cloud of powder filled the air permeating her mouth and nostrils. The nasty taste gagged her. Coughing and sneezing quickly brought attention to severe pain in her chest. She probed her side. Her concerns turned to bruises or broken ribs from the airbag's impact. The deer's body sprawled on the dashboard, its head resting on the steering wheel and its hindquarters almost in the passenger seat. *I need to get out of here. Where's my phone?* Connie reached under the buck's backside to locate her purse. Finding it on the floor, she painfully managed to pull it out. With the door jammed, Connie realized she had to put her shoulder into it if she was going to get out. With each thrust, the chest pain reconstituted her state of emergency. After a few more feeble attempts, her dilemma convinced her to call 911 from her seat.

"911 Emergency. May I help you?"

"I've just run into a deer on Highway 25. I am about fifteen miles north of Dempster."

"What mile marker are you closest to?"

"I have no idea! I just told you. I'm about fifteen miles north of Dempster!"

"Please keep calm, Ma'am. Are you and your vehicle safely off the road?"

"No, I am not! I'm stuck in my car in the middle of the highway!"

"Are there any injuries?"

"Yes. I have severe chest pain. I think I may have broken a rib or two."

"Please turn on your headlights and flashers. We will have someone out to you shortly."

Connie reached under the deer's head to turn on her flashers when she noticed her headlights weren't working. *Great! I have no lights!* The blinking yellow flashes were her only definition from the ominous dark roadway. Feeling very alone and afraid, she began to rethink her decision to leave. Braden's prophetic warning rang in her ears. *Maybe I should call him.*

Connie pulled out her phone and hit redial when bright lights, a semi's horn and the sound of screeching tires pierced the night's solitude.

When the emergency crew arrived, they were stunned by the wreckage. One of the officer's jumped out his squad car approaching what was left of the Mustang. Upon further inspection, he found Connie's lifeless body crushed amongst the mangled pieces of metal and what was left of the deer carcass. The officer turned to the rest of the ambulance crew. He shook his head indicating no survivors.

A member of the fire department asked the officer, "I was told she hit a deer."

A stunned truck driver emerged from his tractor, screaming, "I didn't see the car until it was too late! My God, are they okay?"

Emergency personnel ushered the truck driver to the ambulance for further observation. Once his eye caught sight of what was left of Connie, he lost his dinner and sobbed uncontrollably.

Investigating the scene, one of the state patrolmen reported, "Looks like she hit the deer but remained on the roadway. Those skid marks there indicate where she ended up. She called emergency services at 23:25. Sometime shortly after, the fatal impact occurred. According to the truck driver, he didn't see her flashers until it was too late."

One of the attending firemen, asked, "What's in her hand?"

"Looks like her cell phone. She may have been calling a relative. We'll check it out later."

"Can we start cutting her out of the car?"

"Yea. I think we have our evidence. Bring me the phone and purse when you're done."

BRIAN KENT

CHAPTER TEN

CONTACT

Braden found himself in the middle of a cornfield. Escalating humidity met the impending night air. Together they laid down a mysterious low lying fog. Wandering through the rows of eight-foot stalks, he discovered a tree line ahead. The brush lined a two-lane highway. *Where am I?*

Deciding the stretch of asphalt was his best option, he randomly picked a direction and began walking. After trekking a while down the road, the lack of civilization became disturbing. Other than the pavement itself, man-made reference points were nowhere to be found. Befuddled by his predicament, his pace quickened with his concerns. *What the fuck am I doing out here? Did I have car trouble?*

With every step, the night's ever-increasing darkness weighed heavy on his mind. *I have to get off this highway. I should call Josh!* Reaching into his pocket, he realized they were empty. *Where's my phone? Where is my wallet...my keys?* Panic set in, so he began running. Jogging down the center line, his eyes searched desperately through the endless gloom. *This is strange. No farms...no houses...no mile markers...no more fields...not one single vehicle. Maybe I should stay on the shoulder just in case a car does come by.* Moving to the side of the road, he carried out his hurried search from the loose gravel aligning the highway. His mind raced alongside his focus for roadside indicators, finding himself back in the middle of the road. *Stay on the shoulder, dumb ass, or you're going to get hit.* Remembering always to face traffic, he again moved over until he heard the gravel under his feet. No sooner had he done so when he noticed his Nikes running on the roads paved surface. Coming to a complete stop, he looked down, his feet standing on a white line. *What the hell is this? Was there a turn in the road?* Paying attention to the ground, he deliberately took five steps to the right. No shoulder. He took another five steps. Still no sign of gravel. *Where is the shoulder? Why am I in the middle of the highway?* With dusk and fog rapidly closing in, he kept moving. Giving up on finding the shoulder, he followed the fading centerline of the highway.

Finally, a familiar reflective road sign protruded through the fog. *Highway 25?* Being the only mark of civilization he had seen, Braden grabbed the steel post like a long lost friend. *Good!...Good!...I'm on 25. But... where on 25?*

Knowing the road sign must be on a shoulder, he held the post in one hand and searched for the edge of the road with his foot. The encompassing darkness made it impossible to see anything. Yelling at the top of his lungs, "HELLO! Can anybody hear me?"

Suddenly, a voice softly answered, "Braden."

Spinning around, he shouted, "Who's there?"

Light footsteps approached when a female appeared through the murk. She offered a soothing reassurance. "Braden, you're all right."

He let out a sigh of relief, "Connie! What are you doing here?"

Her smile was a comfort. "You'll be okay."

"I'm glad you're optimistic about it. I've been lost for a while now. Where are we? By the way, where did you come from?"

"Just know everything will be all right."

"Why do you keep telling me this? You're not making sense."

Then, as quickly as she appeared, her softened image retreated into the night whispering, "My heart will always be yours."

Braden was shaken out of deep sleep by the X-Files theme song blaring from his cell phone. He attempted to get up off the couch, but the half bottle of Ezra Brooks he'd consumed four hours earlier weighed him down considerably. Giving up, he allowed it to go to voicemail. With his head still swimming in bourbon, the blurry clock above the mantel shook loose a degree of concern. *1:30 in the morning. Who the hell is calling me at this hour?*

Managing enough strength to get up, he stumbled his way to the bathroom. His curiosity got the better of him. *Dad used to say nothing good ever happens after midnight. I better call back.*

Still staggering, he navigated his way to the dining table. *Where did I leave my phone? It's in here somewhere.* Turning on the light in the kitchen, he found it on the counter. Checking his voice mail, *Hmmm...I guess it wasn't that important.* Just then, his cell went off in his hands.

Clearing his throat, he answered, "Hello?"

"Yes, this is Lieutenant Wells with the Nebraska State Patrol. With whom am I speaking?"

"Braden Cabrera. How can I help you?"

"Mr. Cabrera, do you know a Connie Haberman?"

"Yes. Yes, I do."

"What is your relationship with Miss Haberman?"

"Uh...she's my girlfriend."

"Are you sitting down, Sir? I'm afraid I have some bad news."

CHAPTER ELEVEN

COPING

The next three days, Braden found solace at the bottom of a bottle. The binge turned his apartment into a prison and shackled him to his couch or bed in an alcoholic stupor. With his refusal to bathe or change clothes, the local liquor store owner dreaded Braden's staggering supply and demand. Windows of sobriety were few and far between, diminishing at a rapid rate. He was in serious trouble.

Rejecting human interaction and declining phone calls, his little brother decided to pay a visit. Letting himself in, Josh found Braden's condo in shambles. *This ain't good.* The coffee and dining tables looked like a junk food buffet offering two-day-old pizza, open bags of chips, beer nuts, and a wide variety of candy. Empty bottles of whiskey accompanied overflowing ashtrays, spilling on the hardwood floor. An awful stench permeated from the hallway. Josh found vomit splattered on the wall leading into the lavatory. Ibuprofen, antacids, and his brother's blood pressure medication were sprawled across the bathroom counter and in the sink. The reek of urine invaded his nostrils. He slipped on a puddle next to the commode. The overpowering odor engaged Josh's gag reflex.

He found his brother passed out, face down in bed, propping a half consumed bottle of Jack Daniels against his pillow. *Oh shit! Please don't be...*

"Hey, B? You okay?"

Braden laid motionless, sideways across the mattress as if he had passed out where his knees met the sideboard. Fearing the worst, Josh gave his sibling a nudge on the backside. "HEY!...BRADEN!...WAKE UP!"

Incoherent muttering and a subtle stir drew a sigh a relief. *Well, I don't need to call 911.* Josh sidestepped the broken eggs and Cheese-Its on the kitchen floor to fill a glass of water. Grabbing some ibuprofen on the way, he returned to the master bedroom, "Here! Take this. It will make you feel better."

Braden barely raised his head, slobbering and slurring his words, "What the ...fuck, dude?" He pulled his comforter over his face.

"Come on! Get up!"

Braden's voice muffled through the thick bedding, "Leave me a...lone. I want to...sleep."

"Have it your way then." Josh pulled back the blanket pouring the entire glass of water on his brother's head. Braden shot straight up, wincing, spilling the remainder of his whiskey all over the bed.

Soaking wet, spitting and cussing, "Pppst.....what the hell did you do that for?"

"Its time to get up."

"Fuck you!" he said taking a half-hearted swing. "Get the fffff-uck out of here!"

The right jab completely missed its mark causing the hungover sibling to lose his balance. Josh caught him under both arms and restrained any further retaliation. Unfortunately, the close interaction exposed Josh to Braden's pungent aroma. "My God, B! You need a shower."

Getting Braden into the shower was one thing. Getting him out this funk was another. While Braden was soaking his head, Josh made a couple of phone calls. A team get together sounded like just the thing to get Braden back on the rails. "There...I'm up!" Braden bellowed as he entered the living room. He took a good look at the carnage left in his drunken wake. "Holy shit! Did I do all of this?"

"Yep. This is all on you."

"I'll get to it tomorrow. My head is splitting."

"Ummm...why don't I give you a hand," Josh grabbed the trash can.

Waving Josh off, Braden said, "Nah, its okay. It's my mess. I'll take care of it."

"Dude, it stinks in here. I'll get the living room, but you are on bathroom detail. I don't do puke and piss."

"Saaay..." Braden eyeballed his little brother. "Why are you in such a rush?"

"The team is stopping by in a couple of hours."

Grabbing his throbbing head in his hands, he moaned, "Why?"

Tossing garbage in the can, Josh provided the perfect excuse. "Ahhh… a new case has come up."

Taking an immediate interest, Braden painfully refocused, "Oh? Anyone we know?"

"Yeah, you might say that."

The tone of Josh's voice was a dead giveaway. "You mean me, don't you?"

Josh took a broom to the floor. "We're all concerned, B. As a matter of fact, we're going with you tomorrow."

"You guys don't have to do all that. I'm fine! I admit I had a few too many, but considering the circumstances I think I deserve a little slack."

Josh dropped the broom handle. "Few too many? Five bottles of ninety proof bourbon in three days? I'm surprised you are not in a hospital right now! We know you value your privacy, but this is no way to deal with Connie's death."

"I'll deal with my grief the way I see fit."

Josh couldn't hold back anymore. "How? By numbing it? By killing yourself with alcohol?" Then he went below the belt. "How do you think Connie would feel about this?"

"Well, she isn't here right now, is she!?" The room went awkwardly silent. Knowing he had stepped over the line, Josh backed off. Braden got up, grabbed a beer out of the refrigerator, and marched down the hall. He had a bathroom to clean up before company arrived.

BRIAN KENT

CHAPTER TWELVE

# SOMETHING'S DIFFERENT

The SUV lumbered down Highway 25 towards the outskirts of Dempster. Braden sat silent gazing at the passing countryside. He occasionally took in the small talk generated amongst the others. With Caleigh and Rudy back from their two weeks in Cancun, Josh thought their adventures might be a nice distraction. "So, Rudy, did you forget to pack the sunscreen? That's a heck of a burn you've got there."

The team's technician admitted, "Yeah, I fell asleep on the beach."

"What did you guys do down there?"

"We went snorkeling a couple of times. Then Cal and I took in the cave tours. That was awesome."

"How about you, Cal? Did you have fun?"

"Yes, it was a much-needed vacation. We had a great time."

The small talk concerning the tropical getaway did little to deter Caleigh's preoccupation with Braden's silence. Neither she or Rudy had seen him since he was in the hospital. Something felt different. "How have you been feeling, Braden? Getting plenty of rest?"

"I'm good." His sharp tone notified the others he was not in the mood for conversation. Braden's muted demeanor had everyone walking on eggshells, convincing Caleigh to read his energy. Immediately she discovered a drastic change. Effortlessly, his cognition tuned in like a radio broadcast as if he was speaking out loud. The man was tearing himself apart.

*Why didn't you listen to me? I wasn't trying to be an asshole. Maybe if I would have rephrased my intentions, you'd still be alive today. This is all my fault. I always seem to fuck up the best things in life.*

Braden's self-abuse was breaking Caleigh's heart. His punishing mental state was so depriving and personal that it brought her to tears.

*Why did you take her, God? Why her? Are you punishing me? Are you fucking punishing me? Why did you bring her into my life? What is the lesson here?*

The exploitation felt dirty, as if she was reading someone's diary.

*What is a life celebration anyway? What's to celebrate? Someone I cared about is gone forever! Now, I have to face her family. A bunch of strangers. They'll be gawking and staring, wondering who the hell I am.*

## The Blessing

Feeling like a peeping tom invading another person's privacy, Caleigh reluctantly disengaged, still overwhelmed by the connection.

The four were only a few miles from Dempster when Braden broke his silence, "About a mile up here, could you pull over?"

Puzzled, Josh asked, "Sure. What's up?"

"That's where the accident occurred."

As the SUV slowly passed over skid marks on the road, Josh maneuvered the truck onto the shoulder. Off to the side of the road, stood a recently planted white cross adorned with flowers and nicknacks, the makeshift memorial stirred Braden to the core. Doing his best to get a grip, he swallowed hard and exited the vehicle slipping down the ditch's wet grass and landing next to the crucifix. Someone had leaned Connie's senior picture on an engraved stone, stating 'Another Angel In Heaven.' The portraits infectious smile was more than Braden could take, "Oh Dear God...I am so sorry!"

The teammates gave him a few minutes. It was hard for Josh to see his brother in such pain, but he knew the bottled up emotion needed to surface. Having the moment to himself, Braden begged for forgiveness, pleaded for answers, and repeatedly slammed his fist on the ground hoping the physical trauma would relieve his distraught oppression.

With time of the essence, Josh and Rudy joined him at the crash site. "B? We have to get going. We have to be at the church in a half an hour."

Helping their grief-stricken comrade to his feet, the emotional outburst broke  Braden's silent indignation. He opened up. "I am so sorry. This last week has taken a toll."

Caleigh reached over the seat. "There is no need to apologize. This is all perfectly understandable."

Trying to make sense of it all, he asked, "Why would God put her in my life, then take her away like this?"

"God has a time and place for everything, dear."

"It's a cruel joke! That's what it is!"

"There is a reason, Braden. I know it."

"You want to know what else is funny? The night Connie died, I had a very odd dream. I was lost on a highway...this highway! Connie appeared out of nowhere. She told me I would be all right. I have to admit, it freaks me out."

Caleigh's eyebrow raised, "But it makes sense."

"How's that?"

"The accident occurred on this highway, correct?"

"Yes."

"Did you have this dream before the State Patrol called?"

"Yes."

"So you had no idea what happened."

"How could I?"

"Has it ever occurred to you, the dream may have been a subconscious spiritual interaction?"

The theory held philosophical merit. *Did Connie actually come to me, or was it just a dream? Could it be a coincidence? Was the meeting on the highway her way of letting me know?*

Caleigh answered his subliminal question. "Yes, Braden. The highway was a sign."

# BRIAN KENT

## CHAPTER THIRTEEN


# BLASPHEMY!


he long shadows of St. Gabriel's bell towers loomed over the large gathering out front. The massive stone structure boasted insidious gargoyles doing battle with angelic warriors and a monolithic statue of the infamous archangel blowing his horn from the highest peak. Its mere sight served its purpose, striking fear into those who gazed upon it and a reminder of the struggles between good and evil.

Heads turned to watch the out-of-town SUV pull into the church parking lot. The stares and whispers over the team's arrival soon became obvious, making them a little uncomfortable.

Caleigh picked up on the sentiment, "Wow, they really know how to make a stranger feel welcome."

Josh questioned her analogy, "Why do you say that?

Braden lowered his head, "I'm responsible."

"Oh, nonsense."

"He's right," Cal added. "Many of them blame Braden for the accident."

Sticking up for his brother, Josh said, "Well, fuck em' then. Let's just go in and pay our respects."

The teammates passed the crowd of silent, yet rude onlookers, where they were greeted by accommodating ushers. The church's prophetic message continued inside its walls, housing a three-story altar reaching up to a painted ceiling held up by massive stone pillars. Scenes from Revelations imposed its doomsday story from above with the apocalyptic chain of events leading to Christ's victory over Satan. The bombardment of speculation and judgment made it easy to understand the member's extended mindset.

Seated in the third row, the team sensed hundreds of eyes drilling the back of their heads. The soft organ overture did little to drown out the increased chatter and mumbling. One by one, members of Connie's immediate family inconspicuously turned around from the front row giving the teammates a once over. The ordeal felt more like a witch trial than a funeral service. The foursome couldn't wait for the ceremony to begin.

A young priest entered the cathedral greeting the family with handshakes and offering condolences. Once he had finished, he took his place at the pulpit. "We are gathered today to celebrate the life of our sister, Connie Haberman. Connie was a beautiful, energetic young lady, who dedicated her life to

*The Blessing*

helping others. She is to be remembered for her bright smile, her enthusiasm, her infectious laughter, her countless hours assisting the sick, and her volunteer work, which never went unnoticed. Even though she is no longer with us physically, her contributions to this life will be felt for a long time. She will be missed. Until we meet again."

The Reverend's words did nothing for Braden, and it wasn't long before his mind began to wander. *How old is this guy? Is he fresh out of the monastery? How would he know anything about loss?* His attention was then drawn to Connie's remains. The urn was an enclosed white vase, hand-painted with angels and roses dancing around its circumference. *I can't believe Connie is in there. I guess cremation was the only option. I wish I could have seen her one last time.* Trying to restrain his strangling grief, he sobbed into his clenched hand.

The pastor called for Braden's attention, "...towards the end of her life, it was reported she had found true love. The blessing of passionate love is a gift from God." Pointing in Braden's direction with a smile, he said, "The young man who gave Connie his heart is with us today. As he struggles with his heartbreak, we must pray for him, offering our most sincere and deepest sympathies."

Braden looked to the tabernacle's ceiling holding back a flood of tears. Taking a deep breath, he reached for Josh's hand and squeezed it. A stranger behind him gave a comforting pat on his shoulder.

Members of the family were invited to speak. They took turns listing Connie's numerous accomplishments and reliving days gone by. All addressed the urn with final messages as if seeing her off on a long trip. The memories dragged the congregation into a loathsome frame of mind. Weeping and blowing noses echoed through the church's catacombs.

Braden had had enough. He rose to his feet, "May I speak?"

The service came to an abrupt halt. All attention poised in his direction. A precipitous silence was followed by an encouraging wave from the Priest. Leaning over to his brother, Josh whispered, "Okay...what's this all about?"

Excusing himself through the pew, he stood before the altar facing the congregation. "Most of you don't know me. My name is Braden Cabrera. I'm the man Connie saw the night of the accident. Like many of you, my heart is breaking. However, I know Connie is all right."

The pastor reiterated, "Amen."

With the holy man's blessing, Braden continued, "I'm a paranormal investigator who deals with the afterlife. I know it exists. I have evidence to prove it. I have had miraculous experiences in my life."

The priest cocked his head wondering where this was going. Braden obliged. "I have seen Connie since the accident. She appeared to me in a dream."

Disgusted murmurs broke out amongst the congregation with one man hollering, "Blasphemy!"

The pastor held up his hands. "Grief affects us all in different ways. This young man is still in denial." He then addressed Braden, "Please show compassion for those who in distress."

"I am Father. I'm trying to offer hope and understanding."

Braden's ill-received monitory convinced Josh to motion the team's exit. They passed the optical daggers being thrown their way. The crowd's verbal ousting forced Braden to cut his eulogy short. He followed close behind his teammates. Safe in the truck, Josh was beside himself, "Just what the hell were you doing in there?"

"I was trying to offer a glimmer of hope!"

"Look brother, the Catholic faith does not have a favorable opinion of ghosts! In their opinion, you just called Connie a demon."

"I said no such thing!"

"I know you didn't, but that's what they believe."

The brothers continued to bicker when a member of the Haberman family rapped on the SUV's window. Rudy lowered the glass, "Yes?"

"Hi. I'm Stacy, Connie's sister. Can I chat with you guys for a minute?"

Scooting over, Josh offered a seat. The sibling asked, "Braden, I heard a lot of good things about you. I trusted my sister's judgment. I could tell she was head over heels for you. So I need to know... was it really her in your dream?"

"As God as my witness, it was her. She was all right."

"Did you love her?"

"I still do."

Reaching into her purse, "I just want you to know, I believe. Here's my number. If she contacts you again, please get in touch. I want to know what she has to say."

Giving Braden a peck on the cheek, Stacy let herself out and rejoined her family by the church doors.

Josh patted his brother's knee. "I stand corrected."

The long trip back to Omaha was a roller coaster of emotion on wheels.

# CHAPTER FOURTEEN

# DOCTOR'S ORDERS

The following week Caleigh contemplated the disturbing events which had plagued Braden over the last month. Her ability to read his mind so clearly puzzled the psychic. It almost preoccupied her mind to the point of obsession. They had to talk.

It wasn't normal for Braden to let calls go to voicemail, and the lack of returning them was concerning. Three straight days went by without a response. She notified Josh. Fearing the worst, both teammates headed over to his apartment.

Exiting the elevator, they heard Braden having a loud, agitated conversation with someone from down the hall. Not wanting to interrupt, they placed their ears against the heavy security door.

Braden was obviously upset. "I've told you a hundred times… I can't help you… go away!"

Not hearing a second party reaction, Josh asked Caleigh, "Is he on the phone?"

Shrugging her shoulders, they listened as the scolding continued, "Leave me alone!... You are not wanted here!"

Josh immediately pulled out his spare key and unlocked the door. They found Braden slumped on his sectional. Ten sheets to the wind, Braden could barely lift his head in acknowledgment.

"You okay, B? Who are you talking to?"

Braden forced himself to sit up, slurring, "No one... it's no one. Grab a beer out of the frig."

"Were you sleeping?"

Sloshing his words, he replied, "Nah... just kicking back, enjoying a few toddies. Come on in and have one with me."

"When we came in, we heard you talking to someone. Do you have company?"

Glossy eyed and on the verge of passing out, Braden stared at the ceiling about to fall asleep. Josh grabbed the bottle of Jack Daniels off the table. "He's had enough. Let him sleep. How long can you stay today, Cal?"

"I have no plans. What do you have in mind?"

"His drinking is way out of hand. We need to address this before he kills himself."

"Do you want to come back later?"

"We can't. If he wakes up, he'll hit the bottle again. We need to stick around to make sure he doesn't."

"What do we do in the meantime?"

"Let's get all the booze out of here. I'll order a pizza so we can have lunch. He'll need something to eat. Valentino's sound good?"

"Sure. I guess you know what you're doing."

"Let's just say I've seen my brother like this a few times."

"Does Braden have a drinking problem?"

"He only gets like this when he's dealt some bad cards. I have to admit, his luck has not been good as of late. I guess I should have seen this coming."

"He has been through a lot, but that's no excuse. Pain is a part of life."

"Braden chooses to numb pain. When Dad passed away, he went on a binge for almost a month. I was close to having him hospitalized. Now he has health issues along with the loss of a loved one. This is not going to be easy."

Josh and Caleigh gathered up all of the bottles they could find. Caleigh was astounded by the number of empties. "Has his drinking always been a problem? This is awful!"

"This is the way Braden copes with adversity. Instead of facing it, he turns his back on it with alcohol."

After sprucing up the apartment, Josh wandered into his brother's bedroom. While making the bed, a lump appeared under the comforter. Trying to smooth it out, he found a bottle of Fireball with a note written in Sharpie on the label, "Doctors Orders."

"Hey, Cal! Now he's making out his own prescriptions."

"Well, save it. We'll ask him about it later."

The teammates went room to room searching for more liquor stashes. Straying into Braden's office, Cal found bottles of Holy Water and Blessed Oil sitting on his desk. The porcelain ghost figure Connie had given Braden lay face down next to an open Bible. There was a highlighted passage, "Seek out for me a woman who is a medium. That I may go out to her and inquire of her." She smiled, *Braden must have some questions for me.* Caleigh went through his desk drawers, uncovering a handwritten journal. Curious, she flipped through the pages, arriving at his latest entry dated the day before... "*2:30 a.m. - Chaz has returned. The man will not leave me alone. He insists I can help, but I have no idea how. I don't know why he's here. The voices are back as well. Some are loud. Others seem to whisper directly in my ear. They all want something. Its impossible to sleep.*"

"Josh? Ever heard of someone named Chaz?"

Wandering into his brother's office, Josh had a curious look on his face. "Where did you come up with that name?"

"Your brother mentions him in this journal. Who is he?"

Josh picked up the book and read the entry. "Long story short, Braden thinks his apartment is haunted by a guy named Chaz. While you and Rudy were on vacation, we did an investigation here. We discovered a man named Charles, Chaz, Camfield passed away in this building. From what it says here, Braden must think he's still around."

"Why didn't you tell me about this before?"

"You were on vacation, Cal! Daris and I handled it."

"What do you find out?"

"We had some unusual readings from the wall in his bedroom and captured a male voice introducing himself as Chaz. He also called out Braden's name. Why?"

"I don't think this is a haunting! This resembles something entirely different!"

"What do you mean?"

"When your brother wakes up, I need to ask him a few questions. I think I know what's going on."

BRIAN KENT

CHAPTER FIFTEEN

REALITY CHECK

After watching *Meet Joe Black* and half of the *Green Mile*, the walls of Braden's condo were closing in, causing Josh to lose his patience. His brother was still passed out on the sectional and Cal was dozing off in a chair. Turning off the movie, he thought some Van Halen might shake his brother out of his comatose state.

The guitar riffs of Eddie Van Halen caused Braden to stir. Squinting and batting his eyes, he noticed he had company. "Okay...Okay...I'm up."

Pulling his throbbing head off the couch, a stiff neck reluctantly allowed him to case the room. "You didn't have to clean up." He noticed his bottle missing from the coffee table. "Hey, Josh, bring me a beer."

Caleigh handed him a bottle of water and some Ibuprofen, "How about this instead?"

"Whoa, Cal! I didn't know you were here. How did you get in?"

"Josh let me in. He's here, too."

Josh sat down next to his brother. "We were a little worried. You haven't returned any calls lately. We both want to talk to you."

"If it's about my drinking, I don't have anything to say."

Caleigh grabbed his hand. "I need to ask you some questions regarding your houseguest. Okay?"

"What houseguest?"

"Do you know a man named Chaz?"

Sitting straight up and adjusting his eyes, "Why? Have you seen him too?"

"No, but Josh mentioned your unwelcome visitor."

Braden rubbed his bloodshot eyes. "Yeah. He won't leave! We did an investigation. Elsa did the research. It was startling."

"When did you first see Charles?"

"The morning I had my first date with Connie."

"So about a month after your hospital stay?"

"Yeah, something like that."

"And you've had a dream state visitation from Connie."

"Yes," he responded with a confused look on his face. "What does that have to do with Chaz?"

"If you want to know what's been troubling you, I need some answers. All right?"

"Okay. Are the two connected somehow?"

"Possibly… On our trip down to Dempster, how did you know where Connie's accident occurred?"

"I don't know. Just a hunch I guess."

"Are you hearing disembodied voices? Voices asking questions?"

Now Josh was puzzled. "Where are you going with this, Cal?"

"I'm trying to help. Just give me a minute." Turning to Braden, she asked, "Do you hear voices?"

"What kind of question is that? Are you trying to have me committed?"

Josh butted in. "Come on, Cal! Braden's private thoughts are his own."

Putting two and two together, Braden was not happy. "You've been reading my private journal, haven't you!?"

Squeezing Braden's hand, Caleigh looked him directly in the eye, "Yes, I did. This is nothing to be ashamed of. You are not losing your mind, but..."

Cutting her off in mid-sentence, Braden stood up in defiance. "I think both of you should leave. I've had enough of this!"

Braden stormed out of the room leaving Josh and Caleigh stunned in silence. They could hear Braden going off down the hall. "How dare you go through my things!" Braden was opening and slamming doors. "Where is my bottle of Jack Daniels?" Stomping into the kitchen, he yanked the refrigerator door open. "Where's my beer? Answer me!"

Not saying a word, Caleigh thought, *We threw it all away. You don't need it.*

"I'll decide what I need! Is it in the dumpster?"

*Yes, Josh and I found all of your liquor and threw it away.*

"Well, that's just fucking great! Both of you are assholes!"

*We also threw away your bottle of Fireball you hid in your bed. Josh wants to know what 'Doctors Orders' means.*

Braden marched back into the living room to confront his brother. "It doesn't mean anything!"

Josh sat back wondering if a right hook was in his future. "What the hell are you talking about?"

Caleigh sat quietly in her chair. *Josh has no idea what I've said. I am asking you these questions telepathically.*

Too mad to understand what was going on, Braden turned his frustration towards Caleigh. "What do you mean? I can hear you just fine!"

Bewildered by his brother's accusation, Josh spouted, "Why are you yelling at her? She hasn't said a word!"

Suddenly, Caleigh's telepathic demonstration hit home. A little shocked over the development, Braden slowly turned his head, "What the f... What's going on here?"

"Sit down. Now that I have your attention maybe we can discuss this change you have gone through."

Not taking his eyes off the psychic, Braden slowly took a seat. "What do you mean by change?"

"I think the heart attack and near-death experience has thinned your veil."

"Meaning?"

"Your connection with the other side has been enhanced."

Not sure what Caleigh was implying, Josh asked, "Are you saying Braden has become… a sensitive?"

"To be quite honest, Josh, everyone is sensitive to some degree. Some are just tuned in or pay attention better than others."

"I don't understand."

"Last year, you walked into that lady's basement in Beatrice and immediately felt uncomfortable. Remember?"

"Yes, but that was caused by unshielded wiring. That was man-made."

"It was your body's internal receptors telling you something was different. In turn, the hair on your arms raised and your skin produced goosebumps. It's a biological self-defense mechanism."

"Okay. I can go along with that."

"Have you ever met someone and something just didn't feel right about them?"

"Yeah. There've been a few times."

"That's your energy picking up on their energy. We all have set frequencies. When we meet someone with opposite frequencies, the electromagnetic energy in our body senses it. This is what causes us to be uncomfortable around certain individuals."

"Just like similar poles of a magnet, they repel each other."

"Exactly. Your energy is recognizing or sensing this, thus causing a physical reaction displayed in body language... diverted eye contact, crossed arms, lack of attention, etc."

"So what's this have to do with my brother?"

"Picture two rooms. One room is physical life, the other is the afterlife. For most people, there's a thick wall separating the two. It's so thick and soundproof, you can't see or hear anything through it. For that reason, most people don't believe the other room exists."

Squinting, Josh was having trouble following Caleigh's analogy, "Okay... I agree with that. Most people refuse to believe in anything they can't physically witness. Where is this going, Cal?"

"Our physical embodiment and our energy are two separate entities. When our body gives out, our energy makes an exit or doorway to cross over into the other room. When the doctors revived him, his energy returned through the door it produced allowing his energy and body to become one again. Since Braden subconsciously knows the other room exists, the door itself has become permanent, and will be, for the rest of his physical existence."

Rolling his eyes, Josh said, "This sounds like a lost chapter of Alice In Wonderland."

Knowing she wasn't taken seriously, Caleigh added, "Albert Einstein's Theory of Conservative Energy, Josh! Energy can not be destroyed, only transformed. RIGHT?"

He backed off with the sarcasm. "Yes, Cal. Sorry."

"This is the best way I know how to describe Braden's transformation! I'm sorry if it lacks scientific description!"

"I'm sorry. Please continue."

Cal gathered herself and proceeded with her explanation. "Now that Braden's energy has been in the other room and constructed a door, it will be easier for those on the other side to make an appearance. Just like Charles Camfield."

Braden sat back, quietly taking in Josh and Caleigh's debate. *I hope this doesn't put me in a mental institution. I've had enough bad luck.*

Caleigh turned to Braden, "Yes, you have. But this can either be a curse or a blessing. It's up to you to determine which it's going to be."

Surprised by her quick response, he asked, "How are you so sure this is happening to me?"

"Since your brush with death, you've seen full-bodied apparitions and are hearing disembodied voices. Yes?"

Braden bowed his head in shame, "Yes."

She added to her allegations, "A little bit ago, you conducted a conversation with me without a single word coming out of my mouth, yes?"

"I have to admit... I understood you."

"Last week, Connie was able to deliver a visual message through your dream, yes?"

"Loud and clear."

"These are all the characteristics of a psychic medium. These are the same skills, I possess."

Braden's mouth dropped open. Josh spouted, "Okay...that's a little freaky."

Gently patting Braden on the knee, Caleigh looked him in the eye. "It's okay, Braden. You're not a freak. We just need to make some adjustments. This is not out of your control. I can help you with this."

"Can I have a drink? This is a little bit overwhelming."

"Actually...lowering your inhibitions makes the symptoms worse. It's best to have complete control of your faculties to ward off any unwanted visitation."

"Are you saying I can't have a drink?"

"One or two in moderation is okay. Any more than that leaves you vulnerable. If you get trashed, be prepared for the consequences."

Braden didn't know what to think of the psychic's threat, but Josh was digging Caleigh's stipulations. "So, if Braden gets drunk, he has more experiences?"

"Yes...that's one way to put it, but it also leaves him open for a takeover. Once he relinquishes control, spirits can take advantage of his weakened state. This is why I don't drink at all. I like being in control of my gift."

"You're saying I can control this?"

"Absolutely. With a clear head, I can show you how to turn your ability on and off. It's not the curse you think it is."

"When do we get started?"

"As soon as possible. You need to be sober though. How about tomorrow afternoon?"

# BRIAN KENT

## CHAPTER SIXTEEN

# A DEVIL IN THE CUPBOARD

Braden couldn't sleep. His previous conversation with Josh and Caleigh had him looking over his shoulder all night. The tossing and turning forced him out of bed and into the living room, which resulted in late night episodes of the Twilight Zone and Alfred Hitchcock Presents. The masters of suspense did their best holding his attention; but after a while, the monkey on Braden's back began to chatter. Desperately battling the urge to run down to the liquor store, he thought breakfast might help.

Digging through the fridge, he pulled out a couple of eggs, cheese, and green pepper. *An omelet sounds good.* He noticed the black pepper shaker was empty. Braden searched for the large container to refill it in the cupboard above the stove. His fingers eventually found the elusive tin. He pulled it out, and his hand grazed a glass container knocking it over. *Dang. What did I spill now?* He climbe on the counter and peered into the small storage space. A bottle of cooking sherry laid on its side. The rose liquid had a tempting shimmer, just begging a swig. Braden entertained its possibilities. *I wonder what this tastes like?* Pulling the bottle out, he uncapped it and took a whiff. *It smells...fishy.* Common sense intervened. *How pathetic is this? What's next? The bottle of Listerine?* He placed it back in the cupboard.

A disembodied voice whispered in Braden's left ear, "Sure you can. One or two in moderation. Remember?"

*No, I can't. If I get started, I'll finish the whole bottle.*

The diligent whisper moved to his right ear, "Come on. One glass of sherry with your breakfast."

Even though the omelet needed to be folded, the now overcooked eggs weren't able to draw Braden's attention off the bottle. *I'd be letting everyone down. I'd be disappointing the team and myself.*

The persuasive voice centered itself in Braden's head, "Trust me. It will take the edge off. Go get a glass."

With his midnight snack burning, Braden grabbed the bottle and shut off the skillet. Foregoing the glass, he took a tug. He gagged on its repulsive flavor and spat it out in the kitchen sink. *Yuck! My God, that's disgusting. What was I thinking?* The salty cooking additive shook Braden out of his alcoholic trance.

*The Blessing*

Not ready to give up, the voice turned demanding. "The convenience store is still open. Go get a bottle of Jack Daniels."

Braden placed the bottle of cooking sherry back into the cupboard, "No! Let's not! Enough of this shit. I'm going to bed."

.

BRIAN KENT

# CHAPTER SEVENTEEN

# TRAINING DAY

The following afternoon, Caleigh arrived at Braden's condo pleased to find him alert and sober. After a light lunch, the conversation turned to Charles Camfield. Cal wanted confirmation, "I chatted with Elsa and Daris last night. Elsa gave me the specifics on the elevator accident. Daris filled me in on the investigation. The high EMF readings were in your bedroom. Is that correct?"

"Yeah. Stray and moving."

"Sounds like an ideal location to start your training."

Cal tossed a couple of pillows side by side on the bedroom floor where they both made themselves comfortable. "For me, comfort goes hand in hand with relaxation. Relaxation leads to peace of mind. Peace of mind leads to strength and self-control of one's energy."

Braden nodded that he understood as he mimicked the psychic's cross-legged yoga position.

"Now take in three or four deep breaths and let them out slowly. Close your eyes and allow gravity to pull your body into the floor." Cal followed her own directions by taking a deep breath as well. "Deliberately relax every muscle...in your neck...your arms...your legs. Let your head go...relax the muscles in your face...clear your mind of thought and worry."

She rested her wrists on her knees touching the tips of each middle finger to her thumbs. Closing her eyes, she let out a long exhale. He followed her lead, but it was beginning to feel unnatural. His rational thought processes snickered in his head, almost mocking the position he was in. He peeked out of the corner of his eye admiring Cal's stoic disposition. Her beauty and grace were only accented by her peaceful demeanor. Then he caught a glimpse of himself in the floor length mirror. *I look silly.*

Maintaining her position, Caleigh opened her eyes and looked at Braden. "Silly? Really? Is that what you think of me?"

Braden's face went beet red. He realized his thoughts were no longer private domain. "God, I'm sorry, Cal. It's just so hard to get on board with this."

Caleigh pulled her knees together. "Have you always thought my involvement with the team was ludicrous? If so, I can leave."

"No, no. Please don't. This logical hurdle is something I need to overcome. It has nothing to do with you. I have always respected your contributions." He paused. "I just don't understand your talent. The fact that I can't physically prove your readings is the roadblock here."

With her body language still in a defensive stance, Cal answered his skepticism. "Until recently, all of your confirmations of an afterlife have been proven by meters, video, and audio recordings, which you couldn't explain otherwise. A week and a half ago, Daris picked up powerful EMF readings from that very wall. For Pete's sake, you captured a voice introducing himself to you. What more scientific proof do you need? On any other case, this is about the time you would be asking me for assistance. Right?"

Lowering his head, Braden had no reply.

Caleigh's barrage continued, "You've had personal experiences as a child and as an adult. Do you doubt what your senses are telling you? All of your life, you have chased this. For Christ's sake, you are a paranormal investigator. We've been teammates for over a decade, and now you question my ability? You're not conflicted...you're a walking talking contradiction!"

"Now Cal, I have always appreciated..."

Caleigh cut him off, "I am not just some psychic hunting dog you can pull out of the truck when you're unable to locate an entity! At times, I am capable of gathering valuable information. Sometimes that information is all we have to go on!"

Putting his hands up in surrender, Braden tried to calm her down, "Cal, I'm sorry. You are right. Considering the latest circumstances, I have no right to question anything. I need to open my mind to this. That's the problem. This is all on me. I'm the one questioning this ability."

The scowl left Caleigh's face. Understanding Braden's struggle, she looked him straight in the eye. "I know this is hard for you. I've worked with you a long time. I know how you are and how you think. Unfortunately, this ability cannot be documented. I wish it could, but that's not feasibly possible. I am here to help. But you need to face this new reality head-on. Only you can control this."

"You make it sound like I can turn this on and off like a light switch."

"In a way, you can. But you have to develop this power. Just like anything else, it takes practice."

Braden sat straight up on his pillow with renewed intent. "Okay, let's start over."

This time Caleigh reached over gently placing her hand on top of his. There was a strange energy to the touch, which immediately distracted his concentration. The contact threw his senses out of control. Not sure if he should pull away or go with it, the sensation offered security with a peculiar eroticism. He left his hand in hers while amorous thoughts crisscrossed his mind.

The psychic giggled, "Easy cowboy. I'm trying to guide you."

He slipped his hand out from under hers. "Okay. What's that about?"

"It's your physical self reacting to our connected auras. We'll get past it."

"That was pretty intense. For a minute there, I thought you were going to make a bad boy out of me."

Cal smirked, "Do you want me to?"

His face flushed, unsure of what she meant "I don't think Rudy would approve."

"Not with me, silly," she laughed out loud. "For some, swapping aura can heighten sexual arousal, almost like energy intercourse. I should have warned you."

"Sounds like that could come in handy in the bedroom."

"Oh, it can! But we'll go over that later. Let's get back on this case. Assume your position."

Once the teacher and pupil had reached a relaxed meditative state, Caleigh attempted a telepathic connection. *Braden? Can you hear me?*

Braden laughed. "Sure, I can hear you. You're sitting right here."

Caleigh couldn't help but giggle, "No, silly. Answer me telepathically. Just think what you want to say. All right?"

"Gotcha."

The room went silent. Caleigh tried again. *"Ok, smart ass… can you hear me now?"*

*"Roger, Wilco… I'm reading you loud and clear… Over."*

*"Oh my God, Braden. We're not on broadband radio!"*

Braden seemed to be enjoying himself. The lighthearted telepathic exchange went on for a while when Caleigh went silent.

*"Cal?...Caleigh?..."* Braden opened his eyes to find her staring down the hallway. "What are you doing?"

"We have company. Let me handle this."

He took a look for himself. What he saw caused every hair on his neck to stand on end. "That's Chaz!"

"Shhhhh." Caleigh motioned Braden to stand back. "Let me deal with him."

She turned her attention to the unexpected visitor. "What is troubling you, friend? Why are you here?"

Caleigh could barely make out the entity's words. "You'll have to come closer. I can hardly hear you."

Chaz's shadowed figure sauntered closer and appeared to communicate a message. Caleigh responded, "What do you need to show me?"

Charles motioned her to follow. Closing her eyes, she allowed her meditative state to take over. Drawn into a deep sleep, Caleigh slumped over as if she had lost consciousness. Braden grabbed her shoulders, "Cal! You okay?" With no response, he gently laid her on her side. *Dammit, Caleigh! Don't do this to me.*

Suddenly, he heard her voice in his head. *"Braden. Join me."*

"Join you? I'm right here!"

*"Make yourself comfortable... Close your eyes... then follow my voice."*

"I don't know, Cal. I don't think I'm ready for this."

*"I want you to see. This is part of your training."*

## The Blessing

Braden reluctantly closed his eyes. Even though his fears were making it hard to relax, he forced himself into a dream-like state. Weightlessness took over as he exited his physical existence. He smelled fuel emissions and hot metal. Gradually, the sound of grinding steel and the rhythmic patterns of machinery in operation filled his head. All of his senses were well aware of the change in his subconscious environment. *Whoa!* Desperately trying to achieve visual confirmation, blurry images came and went making it impossible to navigate mentally.

He heard Cal, *"Braden, over here. Follow my voice."*

He answered telepathically, *"I can't see, Cal. Everything is out of focus."*

*"Just follow my voice. Everything will be all right."*

Her encouragement cleared his cognitive vision. Stunned by the transformation, he found himself in a dim lit factory. It was dirty and archaic with soot raising a cloud of dust with every step he took. The massive room was filled with running machinery, lacking human supervision. Its bombastic pounding and full throttle repetition filled the air. The assault on his ears was deafening and made it difficult to hear Caleigh's voice. Wandering through the massive metal maze, Braden looked like a child who had lost his mother at the grocery store. Finally, he spotted her near an old metal door. She waved him over. The sign on the door read 'Control Room.'

*"Is this what I think it is?"*

Caleigh nodded. *"Take a look inside."*

Braden pulled open the door and gazed into a room full of electronic panels. A large toolbox stood in the corner next to an old, wooden desk filled with a stack of paperwork. He thumbed through it. The name Camfield caught his eye on one of the reports. One of the desk drawers was barely open. The single light bulb overhead caught an enticing reflection from inside. Pulling it open, a partially consumed bottle of whiskey sloshed back and forth.

Caleigh instructed, *"Its only a vision, Braden. This is a glimpse into Camfield's life."*

*"So, what is this supposed to tell me?"*

*"At this point, we are merely spectators. Just wait."*

Braden barely had enough time to close the desk drawer before BANG! The control room door busted open! An obviously inebriated Charles Camfield staggered into his makeshift office and plopped down in his chair. He spent some time fidgeting with an electrical component before getting frustrated. He gave up throwing it down on his desk. Pulling open the desk drawer, he retrieved his bottle and took three long swigs.

The phone rang on his desk rang. "Yeah?" Judging by the scowl on Charles' face, Braden and Caleigh were left to assume it wasn't a pleasant conversation. "The part won't be in until tomorrow! We will be without the lift until then!" Obviously upset with the orders he was given, Charles slammed the phone back down on its carriage. He picked up the electrical part and examined it. He dug through his top drawer and pulled out a set of needle nose pliers. The alcohol coursing through his veins made it difficult to navigate the delicate procedure. Time and time again, he worked the pliers into the component. Finally, the needle nose slipped jamming into his left hand. "Fuck!" Frustration set in. He snatched up the part and marched out of his office mumbling to himself, "This will have to do."

The maintenance man stumbled to an old elevator just outside his door. The panel box was open with a jungle of colored wires hanging from its cavity. Charles placed the component back into its proper position. He remounted the unit hastily attaching the wiring. Taking one last look at his repair, he closed the box. *Here goes nothing.* Charles pressed one of the buttons on the panel, causing the doors to slam shut and the elevator to lurch upward. The lift's reaction startled him, and he backed away from the panel. Now uneasy about his predicament, Charles pressed the button to open the elevator door.

A loud CLICK released the car sending it into a free fall from its stable position. A look of horror spread across his face, and he quickly grabbed one of the lift's hand-bars. The car plummeted from the fifth floor leaving no time for a prayer. The elevator landed in its final resting spot throwing dust and debris high up the shaft. Once the dust cleared, Braden and Caleigh looked down at the dead look of surprise etched across Charles' face. His broken body lay in a heap of wire and metal with a crossbeam almost severing his torso in half. Caleigh pulled back. *"What a horrible way to die."*

The atrocious sight did not have the same effect on Braden. If anything, it raised a few questions. *"We already knew this story. What's the message here?"*

A little shocked over Braden's callous observation, Cal asked, *"Braden? You don't get it?"*

*"Not really. This is nothing new. A faulty part was to blame."*

Braden's attention to detail, or lack thereof, concerned her. *"Why do you think he wanted you to see this? Do you think alcohol played a part in his death?"*

*"Well, I guess so. It certainly didn't help."*

*"I'm sure if he was sober, common sense would have intervened."*

*"The poor man was caught between a rock and hard place. If anyone's responsible, it's his boss!"*

The psychic was disappointed, *"You have much to learn."*

The whole experience had a taxing effect on Braden. *"Can we go back now, Cal? I'm beat."*

*"Fatigue is one of the side effects. Just relax and concentrate on your bedroom. You'll be back where you belong in no time."*

.

CHAPTER EIGHTEEN

# WE NEED TO TALK

B oth teammates found themselves back in Braden's bedroom. Braden wandered into the kitchen hung over from the ordeal. "Coffee sound good?"

Cal took a seat at the dining room table. "Sure. We need to talk anyway."

Braden placed two cups on the table. "That was a trip. How did I do?"

"You did fine, but you have much to learn. You have to pay attention to everything you're shown. Entities have a purpose behind the details. What was the purpose behind this vision?"

"I guess, don't buckle under peer pressure? Don't use faulty equipment?"

"Do you think there may be a personal message for you?"

"No. Not really. If there is, I'm not seeing it."

"What do you and Charles have in common?"

"I don't know. He's a ghost. I'm a paranormal investigator?"

"How about drinking? Admit it. The bottle was tempting."

Braden sidestepped the allegation redirecting focus, "What about his boss? Charles was under a lot of stress."

"You know where I'm going here. Don't patronize me. It insults my intelligence. The message in this vision was clear!" She gently cupped his hand. "I hate to be blunt, but your drinking is way out of hand. You are showing the early stages of an alcoholic. Charles was an alcoholic. He may be looking for a drinking buddy."

The 48-year-old pulled back his hand. "I'm not an alcoholic! I've had to deal with a lot of shit the last few weeks!"

Maintaining her persistence, Cal continued to press the matter. "Can you go an entire day without a drink? How about a whole week? If I brought up a six-pack, could you leave it in your refrigerator for a month without opening one can?"

Braden had no response and looked out the window instead. *This is embarrassing. What I do with my life is of no concern to anyone else.*

Cal blurted out, "It is my concern! It is everyone's concern! We don't want our leader drinking himself to death!"

Braden couldn't look her in the eye.

"And I've got news for you. Charles may not be the nice guy we think he is. For all I know, he may be taking advantage of the situation."

"What do mean by that?"

"Remember when I told you that lowered inhibitions could leave one susceptible to takeover? Every time you get drunk, you can become a target."

"Yes, we discussed this last night. I haven't had a drink since."

"Good. Now follow this logic. Charles was an alcoholic in life. Obviously, he can no longer physically have a drink. His need for alcohol is primarily mental; therefore his energy has maintained that need or craving. To satisfy his craving, he must vicariously enjoy alcohol's desensitized effects through the living. He may offer subliminal suggestions amplifying your craving. Once he has successfully stimulated a physical being's indulgence, he awaits the outcome. At that point, the living is drinking for two, which allows Charles to enjoy the same physical numbing sensation."

Intrigued by Caleigh's perspective, Branden pressed, "That's an interesting concept. But I've drank before and never had this problem."

"Your near-death experience changed everything. When you returned home from the hospital, you were different. Your psychic energy has left you open. Charles picked up on that. He may have always been here, but now the connection between the two of you is stronger. Tell me... can you hear whispers in your ears? Someone trying to talk you into doing something?"

Braden's eyebrows jetted upward, "Yeah! Just last night actually!"

"My guess is, Charles is the culprit."

No sooner did Cal make her accusation, a loud crash sounded down the hall causing both of them to jump. Cal grabbed at her heart. "Good Lord, what was that!?"

"Only one way to find out."

The two shaken teammates navigated down the corridor and peered into  Braden's office and bedroom. Finding nothing out of the ordinary, Caleigh put her hands in the air, "I don't see anything broken."

Braden wasn't as optimistic. He slowly backed out of the bathroom, "I do...Look."

One of the dual mirrors in the lavatory looked as if someone had punched a fist into it. Shards of glass sprayed across the sink and floor.

Cal cupped her mouth in disbelief. "Things are getting serious. That took a lot of energy to do that... a lot of angry energy."

"Maybe your speculation pissed him off."

"This should come as a strong warning. I don't think you're safe here. This is malevolent behavior."

"And just where am I supposed to go?"

"Let me talk with Rudy. We have a spare bedroom."

## CHAPTER NINETEEN

# HOUSEGUEST

Caleigh and Rudy's apartment was small but cozy. The woman's touch was a far cry from the masculine surroundings Braden was accustom. Deep down he knew the change was desperately needed.

Rudy ushered him into a modest bedroom containing a dresser, desk, and twin bed. "Here you are, Brother. One side of the closet has been cleared out for you. There are fresh towels in the linen closet. If you need anything, just ask."

"Thanks, Rud. Hopefully, this will only be a few days."

"You can stay as long as you need to. You are always welcome here."

A couple of days passed, and Braden was getting used to homemade meals and the company of others. The family atmosphere seemed to be just what Braden needed to get his act together. Periodically, a drink would cross his mind, but Caleigh and Rudy's presence was an effective deterrent. The living arrangement caught his foreseeable addiction in the nick of time.

At the end of the week, Braden's doctor released him from sick leave and allowed him to go back to work. The welcome news was not only a relief on his drained bank account but a step forward in getting life back to normal. The positives in his life were producing a noticeable change in his confidence and demeanor as well.

Two weeks had gone by when Braden popped through the door after a long day's work. Joining Cal at the dining table, "How was your day?"

She rubbed her eyes before closing her laptop, "I've been doing research. Your blessing is giving me a headache."

"Oh? How's that?"

"Today, I studied various options regarding the disconnect."

"What is the disconnect?"

"Your on and off switch. A way for you to make your gift inactive."

"I thought I already had that power."

"You do, but you have to master it. I've been trying the various techniques all afternoon. It's exhausting. Now I have a splitting migraine."

He positioned himself behind her, Braden's strong thumbs rubbed her shoulders and lower neck, "There. Is that helping?"

She tipped her head side to side. "That feels wonderful."

Braden slid his fingers up to the base of her skull. His imposing energy worked its magic. Caleigh relaxed in his grip. She let go with every stress-relieving squeeze. His digits arrived at her temples and slowly massaged in a circular motion. She laid her head back against his chest moaning with eyes closed and her lips barely parted. Slightly aroused, a kiss crossed his mind. Restraining the urge, he wondered, *What am I thinking?*

Cal whispered, "Don't stop."

Lifting her head upright, Braden abruptly concluded the massage changed the subject. "Speaking of investigations, I got a call today from a potential client in Fairborn, Nebraska."

"Whoa, Whoa. Slow down, cowboy. What makes you think you're ready for a case?"

"Oh, come on, Cal. I feel great. The doctor said I'm in excellent shape."

"Physically you're in good shape."

"What's that supposed to mean?"

"Mentally, you aren't even close to prepared."

"What are you talking about? I've been doing this over a decade."

"But never as a sensitive. Its an entirely different ball game. You're a doorway now. Open for business."

Disappointment spread across his face, "What am I going to do?"

"It's not the plague you're making it out to be. You need more training. I need to teach you how to shut your blessing off. Then you'll be safe. Okay?"

A glimmer of hope returned in his eyes, "Good. Where's the off switch?"

"It takes practice and mental discipline."

"Okay. Let's get started."

"It's not that easy. You need to understand how it works. Your thinned veil is a beacon in the other side's darkness. They know where to find you, and they know you can hear them. They can be persistent, and they don't like to be ignored."

"Meaning?"

"Increased activity in your immediate surroundings. Like the busted mirror in your apartment. Remember that?"

"You mean like a temper tantrum?"

"I guess that's one way of putting it. The sooner you adopt a spirit guide, the better. They're capable of giving you a heads up. Sometimes they can even fend off unwanted visitation."

"So... how do I get one?"

"A spirit guide is your ally. An entity who has your back. You don't necessarily get to pick one out. Your guide will eventually approach you with an offer of assistance. Then it's up to you to accept their help. It's a mutual understanding between the two of you. Its a relationship built strictly on trust."

"So, how long do I have to wait for this spirit guide? How will I know they're the one?"

"You'll know when the time comes. But your initial meeting will be on the other side while you're in a meditative state."

"This is a lot to take in. I didn't know there were so many guidelines to the psychic world. However, this family in Fairborn needs our help. If you train me all week, can I go ahead and schedule the case for this Saturday?"

Giving Braden the look of a concerned mother, Caleigh responded with a little apprehension. "All right. But I think you would be better off leaving your gift out of it this time around. Okay?"

"Fair enough. We need to have a meeting with the team. Okay to call everyone and get together tonight?"

Still thinking Braden was biting off more than he could chew, Caleigh let out a deep sigh. "I guess."

BRIAN KENT

CHAPTER TWENTY

# YOU HAVE REACHED
# YOUR DESTINATION

The team arrived in the quaint village just north of the Kansas border. With a population of twelve hundred, its small-town charm was a refreshing change from the big city. The team passed through the three blocks of downtown Fairborn while a constable sat in his squad car giving the outsiders a once over. Josh had to chuckle, "There's Barney."

The GPS led them to the fringe of town and down a dirt road. Approaching a grove of trees surrounding a desolate driveway, the guidance assistant announced, "You have reached your destination."

"Is this the place?" Braden asked.

Daris discovered a state required address sign laying in the ditch. "Looks like it. Must be up this road."

Both vehicles slowly made their way up the rutted passage past warning signs such as 'Private Property,' 'Beware of Dogs,' and 'Property Insured By Smith and Wesson.' The SUV's rocked and bounced over the uneven terrain. The dense brush gave way to a clearing. Standing before them was an enormous three-story structure, an old barn with part of its roof missing, and a small shed. The house desperately needed paint with some of its siding indicating it at one time had a white exterior. Two of its upstairs windows were boarded up. The eerie look was completed by a front wrap around porch that leaned to one side and had a few missing floorboards.

"Does anyone live here?" Josh asked. "It looks abandoned."

"I see an up-to-date central air unit over here," Rudy noted. "And that's a fairly new pickup."

The team parked in front of the house and Daris spotted utility lines running into the home. "Well, they at least have electricity."

It was one of those typical Nebraska summer evenings, where the heat and humidity made it hard to breathe. As the crew began unloading gear, the stagnant air mounted an assault on Garrett. "Is the A/C fixed in the trailer?"

Daris shook his head. "Nope. Funds have been a little tight since Braden went into the hospital. We'll have to leave the doors open tonight."

"Like that's going to help," Garrett grunted. "I guess if it gets too hot, we can always take turns sitting in the truck. By the way, what is our client's name again?"

"Mickie and Cory Rentzell. They just moved in here about six months ago."

Taking a break, Garrett looked the house over. "This one's been around a while. Must be over a hundred years old."

Still pulling cases out of the trailer, Daris grunted, "Built in 1898."

Elsa wandered over to give her teammates a hand. "It is the original structure to this property. This was all farmland until the town took over. The rumors about this place are legendary to the area. Not sure how much of it is true."

Daris gave her a quizzical look. "Oh. Why do you say that?"

"Let's just say, when I talked with the client on the phone, she was told some rather far-fetched stories," said Elsa. "The reports she received from the locals were quite exaggerated."

Rudy, who was setting up the surveillance monitor in the trailer, Rudy chimed in, "Every town has its urban legends."

The couple must have noticed their guests arrive. They stepped out onto the leaning porch to greet their guests. Braden and Josh met them with hands out. "Good evening. Braden and Josh Cabrera of Paraconnaissance Investigations."

"Welcome to our home. I'm Mickayla, but my friends call me Mickie. This is my husband, Cory."

Cory's was reluctant to shake hands, which caused an awkward moment between the three men.

Mickie gave her husband a nudge. Cory offered a hesitant handshake averting his eyes away as if being forced to comply.

As the rest of the team met the couple, Caleigh wandered around the outside of the house taking in the turn of the century behemoth. On one side of the house was an enclosed garden with a wrought iron fence encompassing a healthy arrangement of roses. A small stone path split the garden in two and led to an old storage shed. Her attention drew her closer to the structure. This caught Cory's attention, "Hey! What are you doing?"

Braden Placed his hand on Cory's shoulder. "She's a psychic, Cory. She's reading the property."

Pulling away from Braden's reassuring gesture, the visibly upset homeowner spouted loud enough for Cal to hear, "Is she going to be snooping around all night? That's my tool shed. It's off limits. There are no spooks in there!"

The entire team looked at each other taken back by Cory's response. Mickie took note of the team's reaction and stepped in. "Now, honey, calm down. She isn't going in there. She's just walking around the yard."

Cory looked both brothers in the eye. "All of you need to understand one thing. I'm not happy about this whole thing." Pointing a thumb in his wife's direction, he stated, "This is all her idea!"

Silence fell over the group. Braden broke it, "Look Sir. If we are not needed here, we can leave."

## The Blessing

Still fuming, Cory took a deep breath and stared at the evening sky. "No... Fuck it... I'll leave! You guys drove all the way down here. I have better things to do."

Mickie tried to grab his arm, but Cory pulled away. He took keys out of his pocket and marched over to his truck. Viciously pumping the gas pedal, he slammed the door and revved up the engine before speeding off. The truck tires sprayed gravel from the rock driveway. A few of the teammate's mouths hung open in disbelief. Josh remarked, "Wow. What did we do?"

"He doesn't believe in ghosts," Mickie admitted through red cheeks of embarrassment. "Even though he's heard the footsteps and the laughter, he refuses to believe."

Braden placed a reassuring arm around her, "If you want us to continue, we are here to help."

"I do. This has gone on long enough." She looked Braden directly in the eyes. "I need answers."

Elsa had a question, "Mrs. Rentzell, I noticed this property was given to you. Was this an inheritance?"

She gave a small chuckle, "That's odd you would ask that. I'm not sure. Cory and I lived in Broken Bow when I received a letter from an attorney here in town. Come in out of the heat. I have it inside."

Mickie led her guests into a surprisingly well kept grand entryway. The cool air greeted each team member like a welcome mountain breeze. The beautiful interior presented a stark contrast to the exterior of the house. Stunned by the polar opposite appearance, Elsa had to comment, "Wow, I was not expecting this!"

"Yeah, neither were we. We have contractors coming in two weeks. The house is getting a new roof, a new porch, and some paint." Mickie shuffled paperwork in a desk drawer. "We were shocked at the night and day difference between the outside and the inside. This attorney invited us down here to meet with him. When we first pulled into the driveway, I thought the house was a wreck. That is until I walked inside. I fell in love with it after that." Finally finding what she was looking for, she offered them a notarized document. "At our meeting, he provided us with this. It states the property, and its remaining belongings were left to me. We've been trying to figure out who did this, but one of the stipulations requires their name to remain anonymous. Weird, huh?"

Elsa looked over the documentation carefully and proceeded to interrogate Mickie. "Yeah, it is. But it's all here. Land, deed, everything. Could it be from an estranged family member?"

"I can't say. I was adopted at birth. I know nothing of my real family."

"Have you ever asked the neighbors who lived here before?"

"According to the locals we've talked to, the former tenants kept to themselves."

*The Blessing*

"Have you ever tried to obtain an abstract of the property? That would provide a name."

"I did! But the records for this property seem to end in 1907." Mickie showed Elsa the abstract. "The last name registered is a Bartholomew Himmelberg. It's all very mysterious. I was hoping your team could help me with this."

Elsa eagerly pulled her laptop out of its case. "I'll get on it right away."

Mickie took the team on a tour of the house. The old Victorian encompassed an expansive living area with ten-foot ceilings. The dark woodwork had detailed, intricate carvings boasting beautiful, and at one time, expensive craftsmanship. This brought the guests to the conclusion that someone had money. The half oval front entryway lead to a grand staircase which narrowed upon its ascension. It gave the illusion of a waterfall descending at their feet. Through the door on the left of the stairway was a formal dining room complete with built-in glass hutches. The door on the right led to an enormous living room with a rather strange stain glass window. As the sun set through its colorful panels, the details unveiled some rather unexpected artwork.

"Wow. This is interesting," Caleigh commented.

"Yes, it is," Mickie reacted. "I'm not quite sure what to make of it. To be quite honest, it reminds me of a church."

Braden admired its intricacies. "It has symbols I'm not acquainted with."

"I know. I don't like it," Caleigh responded. "It's hiding something."

The group continued on their tour, which revealed a small study right off the living room. A wall full of shelves held a few paperbacks the Rentzell's had brought over in the move. Years of dust piled on the rest of the books proved the past inhabitants had quite a collection of reading material.

An enormous kitchen was the last stop on the first floor. An old dumbwaiter door caught Josh's attention. "Does this lift still work?"

"I don't know. The door seems to be painted shut."

"Do you mind if I check it out?" Josh asked with a gleam in his eye.

"Sure. If you can get the door open, I'm curious myself."

Leading the group up the grand staircase, Mickie stopped half way. "I'm glad you folks are here tonight. I do not like these stairs. I've been pushed twice in this very spot. The last time... I almost fell."

Braden looked at Josh, with a knowing glance. "Check them out, Brother."

Josh pulled out a level and placed it on one of the steps.

"What is he doing?" Mickie asked.

"In these older homes stairways can settle. As they do so, steps can become uneven and lean forward. When that happens, vertigo can give the illusion of being pushed."

## The Blessing

"I know I was pushed," Mickie said with a look of disgust. "I felt the hands on my back."

Josh picked up his level shaking his head. "The stairs are level B."

Braden reassured their host, "We need to cover all of our bases, Mickie. You asked us to investigate, and this is part of the process. We aren't questioning you or your experiences. We are just trying to get an accurate assessment of the house. Okay?"

Reluctantly nodding her head, Mickie accepted the explanation. "Okay. Let me show you the upstairs."

Mickie directed the team's attention to an expansive master bedroom. A king size four poster bed rested in the middle of the room with large matching nightstands on each side. A sculpture of an angel stabbing a dragon in the head with a sword stood vigilant on one of the stands.

"I like that statue, but its kind of disgusting, isn't it," Mickie laughed.

"That is St. Michael, the Archangel. He is a protector," Braden reported. "Where did you find it?"

"It came with the house. All of this came with the house. The bed, the nightstands, this statue. It was all here when we moved in."

"Interesting," Braden observed. "Usually, when someone has a representation of St. Michael, they are asking for protection."

A puzzled look spread across her face, "Protection? From what?"

"Evil. The dragon represents Satan."

"Well, that's good to know. I guess I'll keep him right there. That's my side of the bed."

Mickie continued her tour of the upstairs. She guided Braden from room to room. Josh and Caleigh conveniently wandered off in a different direction. Upon entering a young boy's bedroom, Caleigh's intuitive warning bells went off. She grabbed Josh's arm and shook her head giving both of them a moment of pause.

"What's wrong?" Josh asked.

"This room doesn't feel right. It's almost like walking into sludge."

"You mean, its heavy?'

"Despair... Bad Intentions... Curiosity... Being watched... An accumulation of many emotions."

"Bad energy?"

"More like a gathering of energy. It's like spirits muddled in residual energy."

Josh left Cal in the doorway and entered the room. There were plenty of toys in the toy box. A dart board and posters of the Teenage Mutant Ninja Turtles, Batman, and Husker football graced the walls. A twin bed tucked in the corner was covered by a Pokemon bed spread innocently representing a typical Midwestern boy's tastes.

Along the west wall was an out-of-place square protrusion. Josh studied it from all sides, "I wonder what this is?"

Still not ready to enter the room, Caleigh suggested, "Could it be a vent or part of the chimney?"

"Possibly. Are you getting anything?"

"To be quite honest, I've shut down. There is too much energy. Braden should stay away from this room tonight."

"And why is that?" Braden asked catching her unexpectedly and causing her to jump.

"This room is bustling. It may be the focal point of the house," the psychic advised.

"What does that mean?" Mickie asked.

"Cal is suggesting we concentrate our attention on this room. It may be a doorway."

"A doorway to what?"

"The activity in your home."

# BRIAN KENT

CHAPTER TWENTY-ONE

# WHAT ARE YA DOING?

D aris and Garrett had just finished setting up surveillance and were putting the finishing touches on camera angles when the tour joined them in the trailer. Beads of sweat ran down Daris' face as he asked Braden for direction. "Any ideas where the Two-fer should go?"

"What's a two-fer?" Mickie inquired. She gazed inquisitively at all the equipment laid out before her.

"It's two entirely different cameras simultaneously recording video side by side. One is an X-Box 360 camera. It is motion activated and starts recording video the minute it senses movement. It applies a stick structure to that movement, which gives us a rough idea where the movement is located."

"Interesting. And what does the other one do?"

"Mounted on the same tripod is a FLIR thermal imaging camera, which detects variances in environmental temperature. This camera provides a colorful layout of a room. It applies bright color for warmer areas and darker colors for cooler areas."

"I think I've seen this before on television. Does it point out cold spots?"

"Exactly. Not only does it show us where the cold spots are, but the camera also provides shapes and movement when used as a video camera. You'd be surprised what this configuration displays."

Ready to get out of the hot trailer, Daris' impatience with the impromptu Paranormal 101 course grew. "Uh, Braden. Where to?"

"Sorry, Brother. Second floor, first door on the right. I'll let you be the judge on the angle."

Daris grabbed two cases and a tripod and made his way inside. The cooler air brushed his sweat-drenched face coaxing a sigh of relief. Marching up the stairs, he soon discovered he had the house to himself. The house itself was noticeably quieter. *There should be no problems doing EVP's tonight.*

Finding the child's bedroom, he decided the best camera angle was in the corner, but finding an electrical outlet became a problem. He followed a bedside lamp leading to a receptacle between the bed and the wall. Sliding the bed out, he laid on top of it and stretched his arm as far as it would go to reach the socket.

Over his shoulder, he heard someone ask, "What are ya doing?"

With his nose buried, Daris responded, "Trying to reach this outlet."

Still in a precarious position, he discovered the wall socket was full. "Hand me that power strip."

There was no response. Lifting his head, he looked around. "Hello?"

Shrugging his shoulders, he grabbed the surge protector from his case and crawled back beside the bed. Once everything was plugged in, he noticed markings on the hardwood floor beneath the bed. *It looks like the little one's been doodling.* Curious, he slid the bed out a little further. *And with a permanent magic marker.* Not giving it any more thought, he pushed the bed back against the wall and finished the setup.

Suddenly, a loud BANG concussed from the opposite side of the room. "What the fuck?" Not one to scare easily, Daris approached the wall with caution. He gently placed his ear against the wall, but all he heard was the central air unit pumping the A/C. *Is the house settling? It's sweltering outside.* Backing away, he noticed the odd square protrusion. *What is this? Air duct? Chimney stack?*

Daris shrugged it off as he tucked wires out of the way. He decided to join the rest of the team outside. Approaching Garrett with an air of sarcasm, "Hey, thanks for the help."

"I was unaware you needed help plugging in two cameras," Garrett spouted.

"Well, you could have handed me the power strip while my ass was behind the bed."

"What are you talking about?"

By now the heated exchange was drawing attention. Josh stepped in between the two, "Whats up?"

Visibly upset, Daris complained, "I was stuck between the bed and the wall when he asked me what I was doing. I asked him for the power strip. He just walked away."

A confused Garrett piped up, "I didn't ask you anything. I've been down here replacing batteries in the voice recorders."

A stumped Daris focused an accusatory glare at the other men in the yard. "Okay, which one of you was upstairs about 10 minutes ago?"

"No one," Braden reported. "Everyone's been out here for at least a half an hour. You were the only one in the house."

A thought crossed Josh's mind, "It wouldn't have been Cory, would it?" he asked Mickie.

"I don't think so." She peeked out the kitchen window. "His truck isn't here. I'm sure he's down the road at his friend's house."

With everyone now wondering what set Daris off, Caleigh peeped up with a question of curiosity, "Okay, so what happened up there?"

"I was trying to find an outlet to plug in the cameras. I located one behind the bed. I pulled it away and was trying to reach it when someone asked what I was doing. Thinking it was Garrett, I asked him for a power strip. No one answered. I crawled out from behind the bed, grabbed the strip, plugged it in, and slid the bed back. That's about the time I heard a loud bang."

"That's odd," Mickie interjected. "We've heard banging upstairs, too."

"Does it seem to come from the west wall?"

"I'm not sure."

"Is there an air duct along that wall?" Daris asked. He didn't give her time to answer before he turned to Braden. "If it is, the ductwork could be expanding."

"Could be. Let's get out of this heat and see if we can trace the ducts."

Everyone adjourned to the comfortable confines of the old Victorian. They spread out to locate the vents and trace their origins. Josh ended up in the kitchen. Poking around he came to the little dumbwaiter door, which gave him an idea. "Mickie?" he called out.

Mickie and Braden found him examining the door. "What room am I under?" He asked.

"You're under my son's bedroom. Why?"

"Is it the room Daris was in?"

"Yes, it is."

"I think that protrusion upstairs is the dumbwaiter shaft. This door and that shaft are both along the west wall."

"Where are you going with this?" Braden asked.

"What if a small animal is trapped in there? Maybe a squirrel or a rat? That would cause a ruckus."

"There's only one way to find out." Mickie pulled out a small tool chest. She handed it over to Josh. "Here you go."

Josh found a carpet knife and ran the blade over the thick dated paint. He managed a degree of separation between the door and the frame. Freeing the door from its heavily latexed restrictions, he tugged at the small latch. It wouldn't budge.

Mickie handed him a flat head screwdriver. "Pry it open."

Josh wedged the tool along the side latch and put his weight into it. With one shove the small door popped open releasing a musty smell into the air. Paint chips, dust, and debris fell to the floor. Swatting away the annoying cloud, Josh peered into the darkness just inside the door. "Huh? They must have removed the carriage. It's not here."

"Or it's on another floor," Braden added.

"You could be right. Get me a flashlight."

Braden handed his brother a Maglite. Josh stuck his head in the opening. He pointed the light straight up the dark shaft. With his voice echoing from within, "I think you're right, B. This looks like the bottom of the car. Must be stationed on the second floor."

"I'm going to laugh if a squirrel jumps on your head." He turned to the homeowner. "Does the carriage run on a tracking system?"

"Yes, it does. Its operated by a pull rope."

He turned his attention back to Josh. "What are you waiting for? Get your head out of there and lower the car to you."

Josh pulled his head out long enough to ask permission, "Can I bring it down, Mickie?"

"Sure. Just don't let a rat loose in the house!"

He tugged at the rope. The pulleys squeaked as if they were protesting an end to their retirement. A few seconds into the carriage's descent, the medieval operation ceased. Josh yanked harder. "No, no, no. Now what's wrong?" He stuck his head back into the shaft.

Mickie handed Josh a can of WD40, "Here, try this."

He sprayed the two lower pulleys then grabbed the flashlight trying to find the blockage. "I think its stuck on something. Something is loose up there. Sounds like a piece of wood flopping around."

"Dude. Get your head out of there! What if that car gives....."

Braden's premonition was cut short by a roaring whoosh and loud concussion. The uproar caused the shaft to cough up years of filth and filled the kitchen in a near blinding plume.

Braden choked, "Josh! JOSH?"

Gagging and waving their arms, the dust settled just enough to find Josh still standing next to the dumbwaiter opening. His face was covered, except two silver dollar sized eyes scanning the carnage in disbelief. "Whoa! That was close!" he shouted.

"You alright?"

"I'm fine. A little shook up, but I'm okay."

"You dumb ass! You could have decapitated yourself! What were you thinking?"

By now, everyone in the house rushed to the scene. "Good Lord! What the hell just happened?" Garrett yelled. "It looks like a bomb went off in here!"

Josh tried to explain the chain of events, and Mickie grabbed a broom. "I better get this cleaned up before Cory gets back."

Caleigh offered, "Let me give you a hand."

Sweeping underneath the kitchen table, Mickie came across a board. "Looks like part of the carriage is broken." Pulling it out, she tipped it on its side. The corner bounced on the floor. Caleigh noticed a familiar marking, "Mickie, dear … put that down."

"Why?"

"That's not part of the dumbwaiter. That's an Ouija Board."

CHAPTER TWENTY-TWO

# A DOOR WITHIN A DOOR

Mickie immediately dropped the board on the ground, covering her mouth, "Good Lord, what was that doing in there?"

"Good question. It might be part of your problem," Cal answered nudging the board with her foot. "It's an antique... Judging by the stencil, I'd say the early 1900's."

"Oh? How can you tell?"

"Its made of wood... possibly pine or maple. The angled corners... the club and spade symbols at the bottom... and the letters PPF under the Ouija logo."

"Wow, you know your Ouija Boards! What does the PPF stand for?"

"Past, present, future," the psychic replied strolling over to the dumb waiter's opening. "Back then people were into fortune telling. I wonder if the rest of it is still in here?"

"The rest of it?"

"Yes. The planchette. That's the slider the participants place their fingers on."

Caleigh dug around in the debris. "It will be a small wooden piece resembling a heart or triangle. It should have little legs like a table mounted on the bottom. It may have a round glass window embedded in it as well."

"Is that an important part of the game?"

Caleigh's tone got serious. "This is not a game. And yes, the planchette is needed to close the board."

"What do you mean by closing the board?"

"By sliding the planchette to hello, you are opening the board. The planchette is then used by the participants to communicate with the other side. Once the session is over the planchette must be slid over the word goodbye to close the board. The planchette is an extension of the participant's intent. Therefore the act must be intentional."

"What happens if you leave the board open?"

"It's like leaving a door open. There is no telling who or what may enter."

"What should we do with it?"

Caleigh puzzled over it before answering. "For now, I'd like to spend some time alone with it if you don't mind. It may have something to say."

Braden turned to Garrett. "Let's get a camera on Cal and the board seated at this table. Leave the dumbwaiter open and include it in the shot. Place a Rem Pod on the table next to her and another just inside the dumb waiter's door."

"Gotcha. The rest of the house is ready to go."

Josh pulled Braden aside. "Must Cal be so dramatic? She's fueling this lady's imagination."

"To be quite honest, I see no harm in good advice and a fair warning."

"So you think this board is the problem?"

"It could be. There were plenty of personal belongings left in the house. God knows what that board was used for. It will have to be properly disposed of at the end of the night."

They cleared the house leaving the psychic unaccompanied with the Ouija at the kitchen table.

Back at the trailer, both brothers monitored surveillance. "Wow, that dumbwaiter incident really kicked up the dust," Josh noted. "It's going to be a while before the air clears."

The team leader noticed someone was missing, "Has anyone seen Elsa lately?"

"She's sitting in the SUV," Daris answered. "She's living the dream on her laptop."

Instructing his brother to maintain surveillance, Braden checked in with Elsa. The inside of the truck was like a meat freezer. "Hey, its nice in here. What's the good word?"

"Couldn't find anything on Bartholomew Himmelberg, so I redirected my search on this address. So far I have found one newspaper article which is a little disturbing."

"And?"

"Its an article from the Fairborn Reporter dated July 23rd, 1924." Elsa pulled up the saved window on her PC. "Says here, quite a few cats and dogs went missing in town over a three-week span. Most of the pet owners filed complaints. Later, the police were called to a ditch about a quarter mile from here where they discovered the missing animals along with some local wildlife. All of the animals had their throats cut and their carcasses scattered along the side of the road."

"Hmm. Someone had a morbid infatuation."

Not taking her nose out of her laptop, Elsa mumbled in agreement. She continued to scan the screen with intent when she found a related story. "Wow. Check this out. Two days later, a Stella Himmelberg was brought in for questioning regarding the slain animals."

"A relation?"

"Hang on. Give me a minute." Elsa quickly glanced through the article. "Not sure. But you'd have to think there is some kind of connection."

"Does it confirm her address?"

"No, it doesn't."

"I'll leave you alone. You may be onto something. I'll check back later."

Braden rejoined the sweat-soaked team in the trailer. "How's Cal doing?"

"It's hard to tell. She looks like she's sound asleep," Josh noted. "A couple of times her head twitched. Other than that the kitchen has been quiet."

"How long has she been in there?"

"About twenty-five minutes."

"That's long enough. I'll go get her."

Quietly entering the home, Braden tiptoed towards the kitchen. Drawing closer, he heard Caleigh having a whispered conversation with someone, but he was unable to make out a word. "Cal? You okay?"

There was no reply. Edging closer, he called out again, "Cal? Who are you talking to?"

She continued her faint gibberish unaware of Braden's presence. Not sure if he should interrupt, he placed his ear close to her mouth. Nothing she said made any sense. *What's this? Who the hell is she talking to?* That's when he noticed the letter S written in the residue on the table. *Did she write this?*

Braden turned to the surveillance camera, pointing out the letter to his monitoring teammates. Wanting a better shot, he removed the camera from its tripod and aimed it at the scribble in the dust.

Caleigh slammed her hand down on the table swiping across the marking.

Fumbling the camera, Braden dropped it shouting, "Jesus, Caleigh! What the fuck?"

Caleigh didn't utter a single word. Her eyes were now wide open and staring straight ahead. Her breathing erratic. He watched as her body convulsed. "Cal! What's wrong?" He lifted her out of the seat, and her body went limp in his arms. "Can someone give me a hand here?"

Rudy came running. "Cal? Cal?" He turned to Braden. "What brought this on?"

From the floor, Caleigh began kicking and sputtering shaking herself out of her self-induced coma. "Put me down, dammit! What the hell are you doing?"

"You were going into convulsions, Babe!"

"She needs to lay down!" Braden ordered.

Mickie and the rest of the team flew in the back door. Rudy helped his fiancee to the couch and handed her a bottle of water. He looked at Braden. "What the hell just happened? What were you trying to point out in there?"

"It looked like she was trying to spell something in the dust. It looked like the letter S."

Caleigh squinted, "What did you say?"

"It appears you were trying to spell something on the table. It looked like an S."

"That's strange. I've never done automatic writing before. Are you sure I wrote it."

Mickie looked confused. "Automatic writing? What's that?"

Still shaking off her post-reading hangover, Caleigh explained, "Some psychics can write down messages for the other side. They will hold a pen over a tablet and go into meditation allowing the spirit to translate messages through writing."

"Well, there's only one way to find out if you did write something down," Josh piped in. "Let's review what we have so far."

# CHAPTER TWENTY-THREE

# SIE SOLLTEN NICHT HIER

D aris and Garrett headed back out to the trailer where the oppressive heat was finally subsiding to a tolerable swelter. Braden handed over the voice recorder from Caleigh's session. "Daris, would you do the honors?"

"I'm on it."

"Garrett and I are going to set up solitary cameras inside so we can shut down surveillance and begin the review. Give us about ten minutes, and we'll have them up and running."

"Gotcha."

The necessary adjustments were being made when Josh overheard Daris mumble, "What the hell?" Daris pulled off his headphones with a peculiar look on his face, "Does Caleigh know a foreign language?"

"I don't know. Why?"

"Listen to this."

Josh took the headphones and put on them on. He listened to his psychic whisper, "was machst du in meinem zuhause."

His eyebrows raised. "Play that again!" The replay was no help. He yanked off the headphones. "I have no idea what she's saying!"

Josh called everyone back to the trailer. Once gathered at the base, Daris hooked up the voice recorder to an external speaker and played the message for everyone to hear collectively. The short hissing from the amplified recording was broken by Caleigh whispering, "Was machst du in meinem zuhause."

The teammates looked at the psychic for an explanation. That is, everyone except Elsa. "So you speak German?"

"Not that I'm aware of!" Cal answered

"That's what that is? German?" Braden asked.

"Yep!" Elsa answered. "She just asked, 'What are you doing in my house'?"

Amazed at Elsa's intellect, Braden inquired, "So you can speak German?"

"I had to. I was raised in a German household. My Grandfather spoke it all the time."

"Would you please translate this? I know there's more," Branden said.

"Let's do it."

Daris rebooted the recording and stood back allowing Elsa to interpret Caleigh's whispered message. The session troubled the medium. Elsa tried to make light of the situation. "You speak German very well, Cal."

"Gee, thanks. I'll have to remember to book a trip to Germany sometime."

Everyone had a good laugh. Elsa broke down each sentence, "Okay, the first line is, wer sind diese Leute, which is, who are these people?"

Braden tried to make sense of the content. "Sounds to me like she is speaking for someone else."

"Yeah, it does," Josh added.

Elsa continued, "was machst du in meinem zuhause, which is, what are you doing in my house?"

Josh commented, "Definitely someone else."

Not phased by the brother's commentary, Elsa kept going, "drauBen bleiben,

ich brauche ihre hilfe, is, stay out. I don't need your help."

"Were you offering assistance, Cal?" Rudy asked.

"To be quite honest, I don't know. This was a very odd viewing. I usually remember what happens, but for the life of me... this vision escapes me."

"Interesting," Braden noted. "No details?" he gave her a reassuring wink.

The psychic shot the oldest brother a cold stare. "No, Braden! And that's not good! It means I wasn't in control!"

"So this was not a typical viewing?"

"To be quite honest, I blacked out. When I woke up, it was like crawling out of a rubber balloon. It was a struggle to free myself."

"That's it!" Rudy chimed in. "I don't want her doing any more readings tonight!"

"But, Honey..."

"No! No more! I have never seen you like that! If you were not in control, who was? Your physical reaction in there was not a normal psychic response! You are done for the night!"

"I have to agree with Einstein, Cal. You scared the hell out of all of us," Braden added. "Besides, maybe all we need is right here on this recording."

Caleigh reluctantly nodded in agreement. Her head was still swimming in the after effects of her ordeal.

Elsa returned to the translation and commented, "This one sounds like a warning. The next line is Sie Sollten Nicht Hier, meaning, you shouldn't have come here."

Josh shrugged it off, "Eh. We've heard worse."

Giving a snicker, Garrett added, "Like the time we were told to go fuck ourselves in Danton!"

Laughter broke out amongst the group except for Elsa. Her face had turned as white as a sheet. The confidence she had displayed vanished with the next rendition, "I don't think I like this. Ich warne dich, means, I'm warning you. That's followed by, Ich bin starker als ihr euch vorstellan konnt... I am more powerful than you can imagine."

*The Blessing*

The trailer went silent. Mickie cupped her hand over her mouth looking like a helpless victim from a horror movie.

"You don't remember any of this, Cal?" Josh asked. "Was someone in there with you?"

Bewildered and tearing up, the medium apologized, "I'm so sorry. I don't remember a thing."

Rudy squeezed her hand. "It's okay, sweetheart."

"We've got this," Josh added. "Miss Elsa, would you please continue?"

Elsa was hesitant to go on but reluctantly agreed. Caleigh's final message bellowed across the speaker jettisoning a look of total fear from the translator.

"Well? What's that mean?"

Elsa looked at both brothers wide-eyed, "I'm not sure. Its been a while. I could be wrong."

"Nonsense. You been doing fine so far."

Elsa felt compassion for the homeowner, noting anguish in her inquiring eyes, "No. If I'm wrong..."

Understanding her empathy for their client, Braden coaxed, "I know you understood the message. Our client needs to hear that message. Good or bad."

Elsa exhaled a long sigh, "Sie bezahlen fur das was du getan hast, is not a warning. Its a threat meaning, you will pay for what you've done."

Mickie dropped her head into her hands, "That's fucking great. Cory warned me not to stir things up."

"Nobody is stirring things up," Braden replied. "Whoever is here was messing with your family before

*147*

we intervened. Its an idle threat at best. Cal? Have you been able to pick up anything?"

"That's the problem. I think I am being blocked since I have set foot on this property. There have been subtle hints in particular areas, but that's it... that's as far as I get. Someone or something very powerful is in control here."

"What areas in the house have you been drawn to?"

"The stain glass window in the living room, the child's bedroom upstairs, and the dumb waiter."

"What's the last thing you remember in the kitchen?"

"Once I was alone, I sat down at the table. I placed both hands on the board and readied myself for meditation. I took a deep breath. I closed my eyes and began drifting as usual allowing myself to be encompassed by the energy in the room. Throughout the entire experience, I was in a dark fog. Nothing came forward. All of a sudden, I could hear you asking me if I was okay and who I was talking to. I tried to regain physical consciousness, but the darkness had a grip on me. The next thing I knew, you were trying to hold me in your arms."

"Hey!" Garrett interrupted. "You guys may want to take a look at this."

Everyone's attention was drawn to the 42' surveillance monitor Garrett had been reviewing. "The RemPod next to Caleigh goes off twice! Pretty strong signal, too!"

"Huh!" Josh looked up. "Let it roll."

Cal sat motionless at the table with her hands on the Ouija. The RemPod went off again. Daris noted, "Something is in there with her. That room was dead."

Mickie whispered to Braden, "What's that mean?"

"It means there were no readings from any man-made sources. Whatever is setting off the RemPod is not electrical."

"Is that good or bad?"

"It means there may have been an external source of energy in the room. Possibly stray or moving."

The hairs on the back of Mickie's neck went up, "Its moving?"

"Possibly."

Garrett made an observation, "I wish the footage was clearer. Look at all the dust. Its like a snowstorm in there."

"Aren't those orbs?" Mickie asked. "I thought orbs were ghosts?"

Garrett eased her mind. "Nope. Just dust particles reflecting the full spectrum lighting."

Everyone turned back to the footage. The video revealed the psychic's hand gently sliding off the board. Raising her hand, she scribbled the letter S with her index finger in a slow dramatic motion.

"Well, I'll be," Caleigh gasped. "I was totally unaware."

"Whoa, whoa, whoa!" Braden shouted. "Back the footage up!"

Garrett paused the DVR. "How far back?"

"About a minute before Caleigh started writing!"

Garrett reset the video and pushed play. "What are we looking for?"

"Look over here beside the table. Are you seeing what I'm seeing?"

Through the blizzard of dust, a faint shadowed figure developed out of thin air and took a stance beside the medium. Josh loudly accentuated each word, "LOOK...AT...THAT!"

The video exposed the figure standing completely still, admiring Cal's penmanship then quickly exiting the room upon Braden's arrival leaving a trail of dust in its wake.

Josh could hardly contain himself, "WOW! Did you see that?"

Mickie wasn't as enthused, "Dear God! What did I just see?"

"Possible confirmation," Braden offered. "This evidence may have just verified your suspicions."

"Now what do I do?"

"Not you," Braden grinned. "Us. Its time for us to get to work."

CHAPTER TWENTY-FOUR

# GENERATIONAL

The team vests were loaded down with EMF detectors, voice recorders, IR thermometers, Air Ion Counters and mobile full spectrum cameras. The team reminded Mickie of a tactical unit. "Looks like you are going to war."

"Well, let's hope not," Daris giggled.

Braden delegated to the team. "All right, let's do a quick run down. The house is now on solitary camera surveillance. When you enter a room, check the battery life on the cameras. Keep your EVP sessions down to fifteen minutes. Then report in when done. Once everyone has checked in, we'll make a shift change. Josh, give us the update."

Josh reported, "Rentzell home, August 16th. Claims of shadows and physical contact have been reported by the client. Team observations include a disembodied voice, a shadow figure, one malfunctioning dumb waiter, the discovery of an old Ouija board, and a teammate speaking a foreign language believed to be German."

Braden asked, "Elsa, I know you're primarily our research specialist, but we could use your help tonight."

"Sure, what do you need?"

"I would like to do an EVP session in German."

"All right. I'll do my best."

"Good. You will accompany Josh and me upstairs in the child's bedroom."

"Um, Braden? Could I have a minute?" Caleigh asked.

"Sure. What's up?"

"In private?"

Puzzled by the request, Braden ordered everyone to their appointed stations. "Josh, take Elsa up and get started. I'll join you later."

Once they had the base trailer to themselves, Caleigh asked, "How are you holding up?"

"If you mean what I think you mean, I'm fine. Why?"

"No visions? No appearances?"

"Nope. None at all. I'm completely shut down."

"That's good. No energy drain? Nothing tugging at you for attention?"

"So far, I'm good. Delegation is keeping me preoccupied."

"Good. Make sure you keep it that way."

"You sound concerned."

"I am! This is not a good location for you."

"Just between you and me, is there something I should know?"

*The Blessing*

"It is very powerful. Strong enough to block my inquiries. Its attempting to sway my judgment."

"What do you mean by that?"

"Its trying to convince me it doesn't exist."

"Why would it do something like that?"

"This house has secrets... dark secrets. It knows my capability. By blocking me, it thinks its safe."

Braden received a transmission from Daris over the walkie talkie interrupting the conversation. "Braden?"

"Yep."

"You need to come up to the kid's bedroom. You've got to see this for yourself."

Braden and Cal found the group congregated in the child's bedroom. Standing alongside the wall, Josh pointed his flashlight at the floor.

"Check this out, B."

A half exposed pentagram drawn in black magic marker peered from under the bed. Both brothers simultaneously presented an inquiring glance in the home owners direction.

"It was there when we moved in!" Mickie blurted out in defense.

"Why didn't you tell us about this before?"

"I didn't want you guys to get the wrong impression!"

Josh was disappointed in her response. "This is significant, Mickie. This doesn't look good. You deliberately hid this from us."

Mickie stormed out of the room in tears. Caleigh and Elsa went after her. The guys pulled the bed and rug out of the way. Braden shook his head, "This will have to be sealed."

Josh wasn't happy with the explanation. "So, is she really embarrassed or are these two hiding something?"

"I'm not sure. There's no telling what they're into," Braden replied.

Garrett asked, "Do you think there's a correlation between the Ouija and the pentagram?"

"Possibly." Daris added, "The board was inside this wall."

Braden drug his finger across the outer circle, "The Ouija Board is much older than the ink in this pentagram. This is permanent magic marker."

Daris shrugged his shoulders. "Meaning?"

Braden looked at him with patience. "This practice may be generational brought on by influence."

Daris shrugged again. "I don't understand."

Braden shook his head and tried again. "Whatever is in the house is persuading homeowners to open doors. This could date back as far as Native American... this was Pawnee and Oto territory, originally."

Daris looked up. "You can add, Sac and Fox, Winnebago, Iowa, and Sioux to that list. Six tribes fought over and occupied this turf at one time or another. It has a bloody past."

"Absolutely. All six counted on spiritual guidance, conjuring their forefathers' assistance in times of war. Then along came the Europeans opening doors with Ouija. With every gap more spirit could gain access to the property."

Garrett was intrigued. "So basically we have no idea who is here or how many are there might be."

"Correct." Braden felt that his explanation was finally getting through. "Spirits that remained use their influence on the living to repeat the practice over and over again thus adding to the dilemma."

"Just how are they doing that?"

Braden smiled knowingly. "It uses our curiosity against us."

"What?" Garrett raised an eyebrow.

"Experiences, Garrett. What do we do when something happens we can't explain? We look for answers. Once a person deems something paranormal, they may look for those answers with Ouija, seances, pentagrams, etc. The old saying 'curiosity killed the cat', comes to mind."

"If that's the case, you could say we do the same thing with equipment."

"You are absolutely correct." Braden slapped Garrett on the back. "However, we protect ourselves and close doors behind us when we're finished. Not everyone takes those precautions. Some leave the door open... maybe intentionally."

Garrett nodded his understanding. "Alright. That makes sense."

"Unfortunately, there's more to the equation. Within the last fifty years, someone's curiosity took this practice to a darker level. The pentagram is evidence of that. This may be why the activity has escalated. If the pentagram and Ouija have been left open, it could explain the amount of energy on this property. God knows what we are up against."

Josh broke the tension, "Well, aren't you a ray of sunshine."

"Hey, just offering a fair warning."

Regrouping back at the team's trailer, the brothers found Mickie tucked off in a corner with Caleigh and Elsa. "Mick? Can we talk?"

Cal butted in. "I don't think she fully understands, Braden. She is truly embarrassed by this."

"I know." He lowered himself to Mickie's eye level, "I know you're upset. But is there anything else we should know?"

"Well... things have been a little strange," The homeowner said. "My eight year old refuses to sleep in his room."

"Why?"

"He claims he's being watched."

"Has he seen something?"

"He mentioned someone standing beside his bed."

"Could he describe this person?"

"I think it might have been me. I've caught myself sleepwalking a couple of times. In both instances, I ended up in his room. The last two weeks he's been sleeping on the couch."

"Okay. Anything else."

"Cory has been very distant lately. Almost cold. He angers easily… gets upset over the littlest things."

"Has he always been one to fly off the handle?"

"No. Before we moved here, he used to be gentle and loving… nothing like the man you met this afternoon. Something has changed."

Cal nodded her head. "The entire family is being effected. This is not good."

Josh pointed at his watch. "Well then, let's get lights out. Its time to go green!"

# BRIAN KENT

CHAPTER TWENTY-FIVE

# ELSA'S BREAKDOWN

Elsa's comfort level was somewhere between uncontrollable shaking and soiling herself. Refusing to acknowledge the sinister drawing on the floor, she faced the opposite direction denying its presence. She hadn't been actively involved in an investigation for quite some time, and it showed. Her outward expression of fear could be measured by every goosebump.

Josh placed a voice recorder beside her on the nightstand. "There. I think we're ready."

She second guessed herself. "Okay, its been awhile. Are you sure I should be doing this?"

"Relax. You'll be fine."

"Alright. Give me some pointers."

"Make yourself comfortable. The less you move, the better."

"Okay..." She paused and looked around nervously. "Why?"

"These recorders are very sensitive. They're able to pick up the slightest sound."

"Gotcha."

"Speak in a normal tone. Do not whisper. Introduce yourself. Then begin with basic questions. Leave gaps in between. Give them a chance to answer."

"What do you want me to ask?"

"I'd start off in English. Ask for a name. Why are they here. Address your research topics. Ask the same questions in German."

"Okay. What if something happens or I hear something?"

"I want you to tag anything that occurs during your session. If you hear a noise, note it verbally. It helps during review. Are you ready?"

"I guess so."

"You'll do just fine. Daris and I will be in the next room."

Turning off the light, Josh closed the door. "Good luck."

Elsa cleared her throat, "Hello? My name is Elsa. Mickie has asked me to come talk with you. Do you have a name?"

The silence and darkness were claustrophobic. Intimidated by her surroundings, her imagination got the best of her. "Look. I'm not here to harm you or ask you to leave. You need to respect my boundaries. I would just like to ask a few questions. Okay?"

The lack of sound and visual stimulation opened her consciousness leaving her more aware. Her eyes adjusted and focused on the red LED's of surveillance. Knowing she was watched over, she offered a degree of comfort to the other side. "I speak German. Do you speak German? Was ist ihr name?"

A chill filled the air, causing every hair on her body to stand at attention. "The room is noticeably cooler. Are you here now?" She added her translation,"Sie sind hier?"

Her skin was crawling with apprehension hastening her inquiry. "Did you build this house?...Haben sie dieses haus gebaut?"

The unresponsive gaps in between questions unnerved her. The unsettled room seemed to close in. Time and again, she had to retain her focus and composure. "Are you a member of the Himmelberg family?...Sind sie ein mitglied der familie Himmelberg?"

Her fear slowly subsided. "Why are you here?...Warum sind sie hier?"

A tingling sensation broke her body out in a cold sweat. She waved her hand in front of her face trying to swat away the hot flash. Her personal space was being invaded, inflaming her senses to a higher predisposition. The conflicting emotional changes brought forth an internal wrath.

A metamorphosis turned her audacious and demanding. "This house belongs to someone else!...Dieses haus gehort zu jemand anderes!"

"You have no right to be here!...Sie haben nicht das recht, heir zu sein!"

No longer speaking English, Elsa's temperament became volatile. She rose from her chair. "Warum gehst du nicht in die holle!"

Monitoring Elsa's session in the next room, Josh and Daris couldn't believe their little bookworm's sudden change in behavior. "Is she losing it?" Daris asked.

Elsa screamed one last outburst. "Raus aus meinem haus fucking!"

Josh had enough. "I heard that! Let's get her out of there!"

Josh popped open the door and found Elsa with fists clenched at her side. Her attention to Josh, she shot across the room like daggers.

Josh readied himself awaiting a wild swing, "Whoa, whoa, whoa, Sis. You okay?"

Maintaining her defensive posture, Elsa repeated herself, spitting out each word with force, "Raus aus meinem haus fucking!"

Daris slipped around Josh. The two managed to surround the now rabid librarian, "What is she saying?"

Josh readied himself to pounce. He couldn't believe what he was seeing, "I'm not sure. But the f-bomb doesn't sound good. You ready?"

"At the count of three. One...Two...Three!"

Both men lurched towards her grabbing their struggling teammate by the arms. She bared her teeth and tried biting their hands. Her verbal German assault continued amid a torrent of kicking and spitting while the two men carried her down the stairs. The tiny librarian's insurmountable strength was equal to a full grown man. She kicked Daris in the shin.

Josh shook her arm, "Elsa... Elsa, stop it!"

Muscling her to the front door, Daris grabbed the door knob. He gave it a hard yank, but it wouldn't budge. "What the fuck?"

Fighting to keep Elsa in his grip, Josh yelled, "Check the lock!"

Daris let go and tried the deadbolt. With her free hand, Elsa scratched at Josh's face. Daris managed to unlock the door and pull it open. Josh ducked under another vicious swipe before he shoved Elsa onto the front porch. She let out a blood curdling scream and dropped to her knees. An unrecognizable guttural voice emitted from her, "Sie bekommen was sie verdienen." She repeated the phrase over and over again with an obscene growl.

Mickie and the rest of the team, charged out of the trailer to get a first hand look at Elsa's outburst. She resembled an out of control animal as she swung at anyone who came close. Caleigh approached with a bottle of Holy Water. Daris and Garrett managed a full nelson around their teammate's head. Elsa was still spewing insults and threats as Caleigh sprayed the liquid into Elsa's open mouth. Choking and coughing, she spit the excess on the ground. Caleigh doused her time and again until the librarian's wrath weakened. The team maintained their fortified position while the relentless shower of Holy Water took effect. Still on all fours, Elsa shook her head and let out an exhausted exhale.

Josh knelt down beside her. "You okay, Sis?"

From her crouched position, she slowly sat up straight. "Did I faint?"

The team looked around at one another. Josh slowly answered, "Yeah, you weren't feeling well."

Soaked in sweat and Holy Water, Elsa raised an eyebrow. "Why am I all wet?"

"You had a negative reaction to the session. Its over now," Braden explained.

Cal wrapped a hoodie around her teammate and escorted her to the trailer.

Braden asked Josh, "Did you happen to grab the voice recorder?"

"In case you didn't notice, I had my hands full."

"Go check on her. I'll get it."

CHAPTER TWENTY-SIX

# A MESSAGE FROM THE FATHERLAND

B raden made his way to the second floor and was about to enter the child's bedroom when the sensation of being watched swarmed over him like a thousand needles. *What the fuck?* Stopping dead in his tracks, he pulled out his Maglite and did an about face. *Hmmm?* He shone the light around his surrounding area, but found nothing. He shrugged off the feeling and refocused his attention on the recorder. He checked all of the most obvious places, but the device was nowhere to be found. *Why didn't he put it on the nightstand? Its not on the bed. Its not on the dresser.* Frustrated, he pulled out his walkie talkie, "Josh?"

"Yep."

"Where did you set the voice recorder?"

"On the nightstand by the chair."

" Its not there. Are you sure?"

"Maybe it fell off during the scuffle. Check the floor."

There was no sign of it any where. *Did it fall in the toy box?* Digging through the large hoard of play things, Braden felt his blood starting to boil. *Maybe it fell under the bed.* He lifted the heavy Pokemon comforter and directed his flashlight across the hardwood floor. The light captured the recorder's silver cover. Unable to reach it, he pulled the bed away from the wall.

A sharp sting wrapped across his fingers causing the flashlight to flip out of his hand. The luminary ally landed on the floor with such force, the beam went out, leaving him in complete darkness. He bent down. His fingers grazed the cylinder casing, but this only knocked it further out of reach. *Dammit!*

Out of nowhere, the light returned irradiating the hardwood floor like the Vegas strip. Purposely its beam exposed the elusive voice recorder lying dead center within the pentagram.

Braden battled his case of the heebee jeebees and reached for the flashlight. *Come on, Braden. Stop being a pussy!* Working up the courage, he kicked it away from the paganistic symbol and quickly picked it up before making a hasty retreat to the team trailer. His accelerated heart rate and heavy breathing drew the attention of everyone inside.

"What's wrong?" Josh asked.

"Ah, nothing."

"Nothing, my ass!" Cal chimed in. "You're white as a sheet!"

"Just had a helluva time finding the recorder."

"So you found it?" Daris asked.

Braden produced the device and handed to Daris, "Yeah, its right here."

Daris hooked up the recorder to an external speaker, "Let's see what we got."

Elsa's first two questions reaped no response. She frowned. "That's disappointing."

Cal grabbed her hand. "Its okay. Not every question gets an answer."

The tedious playback continued. "Are you here now?" A raspy reply interrupted the recorder's ever present hiss.

"Back that up a few ticks," Braden ordered.

Daris rewound the recording and turned up the volume. Bending an ear to the speaker, Daris listened for the exact spot to hit pause. "Something with an ah in it. Give me sec." Daris connected the recorder to a laptop digital studio and made a few adjustments. "Let's clean this up a bit." Repeating the process, he listened again. "Hmm. Sounds like Da or Ja?"

"Ja?" Josh asked. "What the hell is that?"

Elsa was ecstatic. "Oh wow! That could be German for yes."

"All right!" Josh replied. "Now we're getting somewhere!"

Taming his brother's enthusiasm, Braden added, "Or it could be a part of a word. Let's get through this without anymore interruptions."

The review continued without a response, until it reached Elsa's interpreted conniption. She sat gaping appalled by the words coming out of her mouth. "That's me? Was I saying this?"

"Yeah," Josh reported. "I thought you were going to kick my ass."

"What are you saying, Elsa?" Caleigh asked.

Elsa's face flushed a deep scarlet. She looked at her feet and hesitated. "Its not good. I can't believe I said this."

"Well, you did, and now we need to know what it means," Braden ordered.

Noting the homeowner's presence, Elsa softened the blow. "Please forgive me, Mickie. I was unaware of my behavior."

"Its okay. I have to know."

Elsa loathed the message. "I'm sorry, but the first one is, 'why don't you go to hell?' Followed by, 'this is my fucking house.'"

Cal was beside herself. "You don't remember saying any of this?"

"No," Elsa admitted. "I remember asking a few questions. Then everything went blank. Next thing I knew you guys were all standing around me, and I was soaking wet."

"So you blacked out!" Caleigh recalled.

"Hang on!" Daris blurted. "There's more! What does this mean, Elsa?"

The color left Elsa's face. She shook her head vigorously. "I couldn't have said this. This is a threat!"

"What does it mean?"

"In German, Sie bekommen was sie verdienen means, 'get what you deserve.'"

Mickie was as pale as Elsa, "Who is this directed at? Who is going to get what they deserve?"

"I have no idea!"

"Alright everyone!" Braden called out. "Let's calm down. Cooler heads will prevail. We received a message. Maybe not in way we are accustomed to, but it is a response nonetheless."

"Um, B?" Daris interrupted. He slowly pulled of his headphones. "There's more."

"Really?"

"It was still recording after we retrieved Elsa. Definitely another response... a voice."

"Okay. Let's hear it."

"There's a loud bang during the struggle. That's the recorder hitting the floor. A shuffling sound follows. Then this comes through."

Daris hit play. An abrasive whisper filled the silence of the trailer. "Wo ist sie, bringen sie zu mir."

"Elsa? Mean anything?"

"Huh," Elsa mired. "Its asking, 'Where is she?' Followed by, 'Bring her to me.'"

Braden wondered out loud, "Which one of you ladies is it referring to?"

Josh replied, "Only one way to find out. Send them all in."

"Oh no," Elsa spouted. "I've had enough for one night. I'm going to leave the rest to you guys. I have some things I need to look into."

Braden agreed, "I think we've all had enough for one night. We need our rest. Let's start fresh tomorrow. Mick, is there a motel close by?"

"There's one on the interstate by the truck stop."

"Great! We'll be back tomorrow around noon. Alright?"

"What if something happens while you're gone? Cory isn't back yet, and I don't want to be here by myself!"

Caleigh stepped up. "I'll stay with you. Can I sleep on the couch?"

Rudy looked at his finance in disbelief, "Are you crazy?"

"I'll be fine. I've shut myself down. Nothing will happen. It'll be like a sleepover."

Mickie sighed in relief over the decision. Then she perked up. "Better yet, I have a couple sleeping bags. We can both camp out in the living room!"

Braden yawned. "Fair enough. We'll see you two campers in the afternoon!"

CHAPTER TWENTY-SEVEN

# A LITTLE LAW AND ORDER

Elsa never slept well in a strange bed. Between the motel's over starched sheets, Daris and Garrett's harmonious snoring, and semis rolling into the truck stop at all hours, she was up and down all night. The crack of dawn convinced the light sleeper to start her morning. Seizing the opportunity to have the bathroom to herself, she took a quick shower and got ready for the day. She waited for the java to finish gurgling in the room's cheap coffee maker. She watched it slowly fill the container while her thoughts turned to research. *Who left Mickie the house? It has to be a relative. Obviously someone who knows or knew her at one time. What's the connection?*

The pot of coffee left a heavenly aroma in the air and distracted her momentarily. She poured a cup and fired up her laptop. *Why is the abstract incomplete? What kind of records do they keep in this county? Who lived in this house?*

Her trusty PC produced a half an hour of dead end after dead end. She slammed down the top. Her tummy growled audibly. *I have got to eat. Is there something close by?* Peering out the room's heavy smoke stained drapes, she noted the truck stop's cafe. *Breakfast sounds good.*

She hoofed it across the immense parking lot where she found the entrance to the diner. The sound of clattering dishes, boiling deep fat fryers, and numerous conversations, greeted her at the front door. The wafting smell of hash browns and bacon enticed her to take a seat at the counter.

Elsa hungrily explored through the sticky plastic lined menu. A deep woman's voice addressed her. "Mornin', Honey. Coffee?"

"Yes, please."

The middle-aged, rode hard waitress filled her cup. Elsa asked, "Do you live in Fairborn?"

"Nope. I'm from Pawnee City. Why?"

"I'm trying to find someone in Fairborn. I thought you might know."

"Sorry. Not from around here. But Sheriff Steincamp usually rolls in here about this time. He may be able to help you."

"Great. I'll look for him."

"Are you ready to order?"

"Yes. I'll have the biscuits and gravy with a side of hash browns and a couple strips of bacon."

"I'll have it right out to you."

"Thank you," Elsa smiled.

## The Blessing

Elsa's breakfast arrived a few minutes later. Steam rolled off the plate and the aroma of the food filled her with even more longing to eat. She wasted no time cleaning her plate. She was nibbling on her last few bites of bacon when the waitress returned. "My, my. You were hungry. Just thought I'd let you know, the sheriff and his deputy just walked in. They're in that booth right over there."

"Great," Elsa replied. "Can I get my check?"

"You go on over, Hon. I'll bring it to you."

Elsa grabbed her cup of coffee and headed over to the constable's booth. "Good morning! Sheriff Steincamp?"

Being a respectable gentleman, the tall, pot bellied officer struggled to stand in the booth's tight quarters. "Yes, Ma'am." He said with a smile. "How can I help?"

"My name is Elsa Burk, and I'm with Paraconnaissance Investigations. Do you have a minute, Sir?"

"By all means, have a seat."

Elsa crowded in next to the sheriff. "I'm working on a case here in Fairborn, and I'm trying to locate a name for a property."

"Just a minute." The lawman asked, "Are you a private investigator?"

"No, Sir. I'm a paranormal investigator."

The deputy across the table got a big smirk on his face. He giggled. "You mean like a ghostbuster?"

Rolling her eyes in disgust, she answered, "Yeah, like I've never heard that before."

The sheriff tempered his surrogate's insensitive gesture. "Just hang on now, Kyle. I happen to believe in spirits." Turning back to Elsa, he asked, "What property are you looking into?"

"The farm on the east edge of Fairborn. The one kind of tucked away off of county road six."

The sheriff scratched his head. "Seems to me there are two families just east of Fairborn on county road six. The Bischoff's and the Himmelberg's."

Elsa's eyes got as big as the lawman's arriving plate of breakfast, "Did you say Himmelberg?"

He anxiously grabbed his meal from the waitress. "Yeah. That property has been in their family for generations, long before I was born."

A light bulb went off in Elsa's head. "That's why!"

"That's why, what?" the sheriff asked, dousing his eggs in Tabasco sauce.

Elsa jumped up from her seat. "Thank you, Sheriff! You've been a big help!"

Hardly able to contain herself, she made a dash for the exit and almost forgot to pay her check. She returned to the register and handed the cashier a twenty. "Give the rest to my waitress!"

Returning to the motel room, she found Garrett shaving and Daris flicking through TV channels. "Where have you been?"

Elsa appeared almost giddy. "I'm pretty sure I know who owned the house before the Rentzells!"

Daris shut off the TV and gave her his full attention. "Okay? Who's that?"

## The Blessing

"The reason the property's abstract has not been adjusted since 1907 is because its never left the family! According to the sheriff, Mickie's property is known as the Himmelberg farm! Its been passed on from generation to generation!"

Wiping the excess shaving cream from his face, Garrett added, "Possibly making Mickie a Himmelberg."

"Exactly!" Elsa shouted. "But how do we make the connection?"

"Well, if she is a Himmelberg," the retired detective replied, "she may have been born here."

"We need access to records," Elsa noted. "Nothing online is coming up, and its Sunday. All county and city buildings are closed."

An all-knowing smile snuck under Garrett's handlebar mustache. "That old hospital we passed is open."

Dumbfounded, Daris muttered, "Yeah? So?"

"These small town hospitals are lucky to have a birth once a month. All we need is Mickie's date of birth, and we might be able to trace it to this hospital. Maybe even get the name of her birth mother."

"And what makes you think they are just going to hand over records like that?"

Garrett got a gleam in his eye. "You just let me handle that part."

As soon as Daris and Garrett finished cleaning up, the three made their way to Fairborn's only medical facility. Built sometime in the fifties, the old building

175

looked as if it had gone through numerous expansions and renovations in order to stay in operation. Garrett turned to his colleagues as they passed through the revolving door. "You two stay right here in the waiting area. I'll be back."

Garrett waltzed down the hall looking for assistance. An older nurse greeted him. "Can I help you, Sir."

He stood straight and pulling out his wallet. "Yes, Ma'am." He flashed his retired badge. "Officer Rodgers with the Omaha Police Department. I'm working on a cold case and need to review some records. Where do I need to go?"

Somewhat smitten by the old lawman's good looks, the nurse took him personally to the hospital records department. "So is it a murder you're looking into?"

He kept up his Wyatt Earp charade. "No, Ma'am. Trying to locate someone's birth place. The poor girl has amnesia. We're assisting the investigation."

Enamored by his canter, the aid was more than willing to assist. "Our records are very well kept. We should be able to find what you are looking for."

She led him into a room full of file cabinets. "Approximately what time period are we looking at?"

Clearing this throat, he pulled out a piece of paper, "February 12th, 1982 to be exact."

"And you said a baby girl, correct?"

"Yes, Ma'am."

The staff member momentarily left Garrett alone. He was astonished by her cooperation. *Like taking candy from a baby.* The nurse returned with a file in hand and a smile on her face. "I believe we may have found your young lady, Officer. A baby girl was delivered on that date in this facility. Her name is Mickayla Ann."

"Mickayla Ann who?"

"I'm sorry, Officer. But that information is deemed classified."

"Classified? Why is it classified?"

"Mickayla was set up for adoption upon birth. Her mother was only 16 years old, making her a minor. There are laws protecting a minor's privacy. I'm sure you understand."

"Well, that doesn't help."

"Look, Officer Rodgers, you asked for a name. That is all I can give you."

"Well, can I at least have the mother's address at the time of Mickayla's birth?"

Noting the desperation in Garrett's eye, the nurse let out a sigh. "I guess there's no harm in that. The mother moved a long time ago." Reopening the file, "618 County Road 6."

Feeling his charm had ran its course, Garrett nodded to his informant with a wink. "Thank you, Ma'am. You've been a big help!"

Garrett returned to his anxiously awaiting teammates. "I think we may have solved one mystery!"

All three, practically danced out of the hospital. It was going to be one interesting day on the farm.

# CHAPTER TWENTY-EIGHT

# A TRUCE

Braden, Josh, and Rudy were the first to return. They found Caleigh and Mickie lounging out front sipping ice tea. Cory's red pick up caught all three of the investigator's attention. "Great. Mister congeniality is back."

"Now, Josh. Its his house."

Braden joined the girls on the front lawn. "Everyone sleep well?" he asked.

"As well as could be expected," Caleigh replied. "We were woke up around 3:30 by a loud bang. Not sure if it was paranormal or not. It could have been Mickie's husband coming home."

"Okay. How is he doing today?"

"He seemed to be fine this morning. A little hungover. He still thinks this a big waste of time. He went out hunting last night with his buddies. He's out in the barn right now," Mickie reported.

"Do you think it would be a good idea for me to chat with him? Maybe smooth things over?"

"I don't know. I guess it wouldn't hurt. If I were you, I would announce myself before you enter the barn."

"Good point. Josh, Rudy? Why don't you two start review of last night's surveillance. I'll negotiate a truce."

Braden made his way across the weed infested farm yard towards the dilapidated structure. The heat and humidity drew mosquitoes turning Braden's exposed appendages into a smorgasbord. He swatted them away as he trudged onward. Not far from the structure an offensive odor invaded his nostrils. *Good Lord. What the hell is that?* He called out, "Mr. Rentzell? Are you out here?"

There was no reply. "Mr. Rentzell? Its Braden Cabrera! Can we talk for a minute?"

Cory stepped out of the barn's shadowed doorway, a large butcher's knife in hand. "What do you want?"

Not sure whether to take another step, Braden froze with his hands in the air. "I just want to talk."

Cory thoroughly enjoyed Braden's surrendered stance. A condescending smirk spread across Cory's face. "Oh, what the hell. Come on back!"

Braden cautiously entering the foreboding barn. He was greeted with a repulsive stench, accompanied by a swarm of flies. He covered his nose and mouth. His gag reflexes induced an upset stomach. Dodging several low hanging extension cords, he followed the sound of a humming generator.

From somewhere in the distance Cory yelled, "I'm back here."

## The Blessing

Braden followed the shout to a dimly lit room.

Braden found Cory standing ankle deep in blood and entrails, disemboweling a fresh kill. Braden did his best not to regurgitate at the sight.

Reaching into the animal's lower abdomen, Cory pulled out the deer's intestinal tract allowing it to drop on the ground in a horrific splat. The digestive tract continued to stream out of the carcass like a runaway train. At that point Braden purged everything in his stomach much to the delight of his carnivorous host.

Cory giggled with bogus concern. "This is always the worst part. You okay?"

Braden wiped his chin and retreated from a crouched position. He was not about to afford Cory the last laugh. "Looks like venison at the Rentzell home, tonight."

Both men broke out in laughter, which broke the ice. Cory pointed his knife out the door. "Head on out to the truck. Grab a beer out of the cooler. I'll be out shortly."

Cory emerged from the barn to find Braden sitting on his truck's tailgate. "My God! What did you have for breakfast? It stinks in there!"

Popping open a couple of Budweisers, the two exchanged small talk for a while. Eventually the conversation reverted to the house. With tensions eased, Braden dropped the kid gloves and addressed the issue at hand. "You know... not everybody believes in ghosts. And that's okay. To be quite honest, I myself am skeptical of every location until it proves itself otherwise."

"I can respect that, Braden. But you must understand one thing. We have nowhere else to go. We have to live here. If this place has spooks or whatever, we'll have to deal with it. I'm concerned this investigation of yours is going to make matters worse. Stir things up! Then what do we do?"

Braden thought out his reply carefully. "So, if I'm understanding you correctly, your solution is to ignore the problem and hope it leaves on its own?"

"Exactly." Cory took another tug off his beer. "If we don't pay attention to it, it'll give up."

Braden chose his words cautiously. "What if that doesn't work?"

Cory stood up looking Braden straight in the eye. "I told you yesterday… I don't believe in ghosts."

"Then there should be nothing to be afraid of. Right?"

Braden's comeback forced Cory to withdrawal his defensive. Knowing he had Cory on the ropes, Braden added, "Follow me, brother. You need to see something."

Braden invited Cory to the trailer and sat him down in front of the team's 42 inch monitor. He showed the incredulous farm owner the previous evening's evidence. As he was watching, Daris, Garrett, and Elsa returned from their successful fact finding mission.

"Nice to see you could join us," Josh spouted. "We're finished with the overnight review."

"Sorry," Garrett boasted, "but we we've been busy looking into our client's origins."

That caught everyone's attention. Braden paused Cory's reveal. "Did you find anything?"

"Yes sir! It appears Mickie is a local girl after all."

"Can we get out of this heat?" Mickie asked. "I don't want to faint when I hear this."

Once everyone had congregated in the Rentzell's living room, Elsa laid out the chain of events. "This is still considered the Himmelberg family farm. The property's been in their family for at least four to five generations. This is why the abstract was never been changed."

Cory suddenly showed interest. "Legally aren't they supposed to include a first and last name for each transfer?"

"You would think," Elsa replied. "My guess is the latest modification will only show a date for Mickie's acquisition. Its been done that way for years"

A wave of emotion rolled over Mickie, "So... my birth name is Himmelberg? Mickayla Himmelberg?"

"We believe so," Garrett surmised. "According to hospital records, a baby girl named Mickayla Ann was born on your birthday in Fairborn Memorial. That child was given up for adoption upon birth."

Cal handed Mickie a Kleenex. "Did they say why?"

"The mother was only sixteen at the time. The aid would not divulge anymore information. However, records did list this address as that of the mother."

Almost sobbing, Mickie uttered, "So, is my birth mother dead?"

"I'll see what I can do. Now that I have some new numbers, I may be able to narrow things down," Elsa perceived.

Admiring the detective work, Cory exhibited a genuine smile. "Wow! There is more to this ghost hunting than I could imagine. Great job, guys!"

"And we're just getting started," Braden boasted. "This research has raised a lot of questions. Tonight's EVP sessions should be anything but boring."

.

CHAPTER TWENTY-NINE

# THE ONE ON ONE

With a full moon lurking just over the horizon, expectations were high. No one wanted to miss a single opportunity. Last minute tactical adjustments were being made. Daris increased the amount of infrared illumination throughout the Victorian, while Braden and Josh added more surveillance. They practically covered every square inch of the house.

Now on board, Cory offered assistance by relaying equipment to the second level. "Garrett said you'd want these. What are they?"

Josh opened the case, "EMF data loggers. They detect EMF surges, time stamping the spikes. The lights on top signal the increase as it passes over."

"Interesting. Where do you want them?"

"If you don't mind, we need those evenly spaced up and down the grand staircase."

"Will do."

Down in the kitchen, Mickie and Caleigh were preparing snacks. The latest developments and amped up investigation weighed on Mickie's mind. "So, what's the game plan for tonight?"

"The team thinks a one-on-one is necessary."

"One-on-one? What's that?"

"The client is left alone in the location while under surveillance. You will ask the questions in a private EVP session."

Mickie stopped chopping celery. "Oh, hell no!"

"Now, dear. This is your home. I have a gut feeling whoever is in here wants to talk with you. It could be a relative... maybe your mother."

"What do I ask? What if it does the same thing to me that it did to you and Elsa?"

"I have strong suspicions it won't. We are strangers. You are not. This house was given to you for a reason. The answers you have sought since birth could be revealed. You owe this to yourself."

"I guess you're right."

"You'll be fine. We'll be monitoring the entire process from the trailer."

"So, when will this go down?"

"As soon as the guys finish up."

After a light dinner, everyone gathered in the living room. Not one to take protection lightly, Braden began blessing each teammate. As he approached Mickie and Cory with the vial of Holy Oil, a sharp stabbing pain in his fingers caused him to drop the bottle on the floor. *What the hell?*

Josh picked up the bottle for his brother. "Got a case of the oopsies today?"

"Nah, just got a cramp."

Braden took the bottle from Josh and finished the process. He gave one final pep talk. "Alright, we have a lot of ground to cover. I want to start with Mickie's one-on-one. We're going to give her thirty minutes to address as many questions as possible. Afterward we'll review her session and go from there. Cal? Would you take Mickie in and get her situated?"

"Same room?" the psychic asked.

"No. Get her comfortable in her own bedroom. That way Saint Mike can keep an eye on her."

"But B, almost all of the activity is in the other room!" Josh spouted.

"Exactly. I want this session to test boundaries. That statue of Saint Michael was left here for a reason. If it does offer protection, that could provide some insight."

Cal escorted Mickie up to the pitch black master bedroom. Mickie's reluctance doubled her heart rate and turned her legs into rubber. "I don't know if I can do this!"

Cal guided the home owner by one arm. "You will be fine. Just ask the questions you need to ask. Speak from the heart. I'll be watching from right outside."

"How can you see anything? Its so dark in here!"

"Sweet pea, you need to calm down. See those red lights in the corner? That's the surveillance. That is us watching over you."

Caleigh led her to the bed, handed her a flashlight, and propped her head up with an extra pillow. "Comfy?"

"I guess."

"Here's a walkie talkie. Use it only in case of emergency. The voice recorder is running. You can start whenever you're ready."

"How about tomorrow in broad daylight?"

Once Cal slipped out of the room, the session began.

"Hello?... Whoever you are... Can I have a name?"

Mickie shifted her seated position causing the old bed to creak and moan like an old horror movie sound effect.

"I'd like to know who left me this house. Are you that person?"

Mickie gazed at Saint Michael. "Did you leave me this statue?"

Mickie found the one-sided conversation became easier with each question. "Look. I don't speak German. If you need to say something, you'll have to tell me in English. Are you a relative? Are you my Mother?"

Mickie fought back a tear. "If you are my Mother, why did you put me up for adoption?"

"Just so you know, my adopted family was very good to me."

With increased fortitude, she focused on details. "Did you draw that pentagram on the floor in the other room?

"Was that your Ouija Board in the dumbwaiter?"

"Were you down in the kitchen with Caleigh?"

"What did you do to Elsa yesterday? Why did you do that?"

"Who pushed me on the stairs?"

"Is there more than one of you?"

Mickie's pupils widened as she grew accustomed to the darkness. She was able to make out subtle details. Her eyes caught a disconsolate figure standing at the doorway. "Hello?"

Squinting and blinking in disbelief, she begged it to be a figment of her imagination. Her prayers went unanswered. The form remained and moved along the wall gaining height and mass. Stricken with fear, every muscle in Mickie's body stiffened rendering her paralyzed. The alleged menace drew closer. It seemed to be inquisitive of the homeowner's reaction. Mickie struggled to scream. Her inability to exhale left her on the verge of passing out. She lost control of her bladder in the process. The ominous shadow advanced to the opposite side of the bed taking a seat. Mickie could feel the mattress compress under its weight.

Her vocal cords cut loose a horrific, "LEAVE ME ALONE!"

Adrenalin shot through her body releasing her from the fear induced chains. Mickie leaped from the bed and ran for the door and down the stairs. Cory and the team rushed to her as she shoved the front door wide open. Hyperventilating, she ran to her husband's arms unable to control herself. Cory held her close. "Its okay now. Its okay. Calm down."

Shaking her head, Mickie spouted between gasps, "Its… in… there! I… saw… it!"

Cory wasn't happy. "See what I mean? I told you this would happen. Its getting worse since you've been involved."

"Nonsense," Caleigh reiterated. "It was here way before we arrived. It wants to be heard."

Still holding his trembling wife, Cory said, "That may be true, but you have to admit the occurrences have intensified since your arrival."

Caleigh stood her ground. "Do you know why?… I'll tell you. It knows why we are here. It understands our intentions, and it knows we are trying to understand its intentions!"

Cory refused to back down. "It is my understanding you and your team were threatened! Shouldn't that tell you something?"

"Absolutely!" Caleigh's voice got louder. "But we don't run away from threats. This is not something you can ignore and hope it goes away. The fact that it did make a threat only proves its malicious and is hiding something. Look what's been uncovered in two days."

Unable to deny Caleigh's allegations, the deliberation went into a ceasefire, which left Cory at a loss for words.

Caleigh closed her eyes and took a few deep breaths to gather her composure. Slowly her eyes reopened, and the psychic lowered her tone. "We've established a presence in this house. We have confirmed and are validating you and your wife's suspicions; however, we have yet to discover its intent. We have reason to believe it is trying to cover its tracks. Has it been taking advantage of its situation? Possibly. Something tried to push your wife down the stairs. Something succeeded in controlling Elsa and me. Something frightened your wife not more than fifteen minutes ago. Its here... In order to rectify the problem, we need to understand its motive."

Mickie added, "Well, I'm all for that, but I'm not going back in there to ask!"

Cal assured her, "You've already done your part. Let's review your session."

# BRIAN KENT

CHAPTER THIRTY

# STEPPING UP TO THE PLATE

A disheartening half an hour of review revealed nothing. To make matters worse, Mickie's black mass could not be documented on surveillance.

Disappointment seeped through Josh's voice. "I can't believe it! After all that we are left with an empty bag!"

Caleigh saw it differently. "You're missing the big picture."

"How's that?"

"Only Mickie has seen the mass. Obviously its message is for her, and her alone."

"We get that," Daris replied. "But how the hell was it able to go undetected under full spectrum surveillance? We caught it yesterday!"

"Its a quick learner. It knows our intentions. The fact that it left no trace proves it understands the equipment and possibly even how to manipulate it. This is definitely an intelligent entity."

Garrett wasn't buying it. "So you're saying this spirit is able to camouflage itself? That's preposterous! Nothing can escape full spectrum."

Josh added, "Exactly! An entity this strong has to produce some kind of energy trace or illuminant vacuum."

Daris noted, "Mickie claimed it tried crawling in bed, but the RemPod sitting next to her never went off."

Cory's temper reappeared. "Are you saying her imagination got the best of her?"

Caleigh was not appreciating the closed minded candor of the conversation. "Will all of you stop with the scientific theory! Do any of us truly understand how the other side works? No! I told you on day one this house has many secrets... dark secrets. Whatever is in this house has been able to keep those secrets under wrap for years! It has its own agenda and has been carrying it out for a long time! Its able to be conspicuous whenever it wants. Then it goes into hiding at a moment's notice. You honestly didn't believe you were going to outsmart it with a few cameras, meters, and voice recorders, did you?"

Caleigh's rant left the trailer silent. Frustrated, she stormed out into the yard.

Braden followed her. "Cal? Don't be mad. We're all on the same team here with the same goal."

"Oh, I'm not mad at them. I feel helpless, and this case is at a dead end... No pun intended."

"We've made great strides this weekend. There is nothing to be ashamed of."

"All we have done is validate the haunt and provide Mickie with an, at best, speculative family history."

Braden knew she was right. He lit up a smoke and pondered the team's next move. "Well... normally in this situation you would do a reading."

"Well, that's not going to happen. Rudy threatened to leave me if I do anymore readings in this house."

"Okay... but I could give it a shot."

Caleigh grabbed his arm. "Don't you dare! This energy is way out of your league!"

He took a long drag off his Marlboro before answering. "Last time I checked, I am this team's leader. If it'll help, I see no reason why I shouldn't step up to the plate. I've practically been on the sidelines this entire weekend."

Cal held onto him with a hand on each of his shoulders and looked him directly in the eyes. "Please tell me you are not seriously contemplating this! You have no idea what you're getting into. For the love of God, it was able to control me... There's no telling what it will do to you!"

"There's only one way to find out. We need a reading, and I'm going to do it. The decision's been made."

Cal looked at him directly in the eye. "You don't have to do this. Let's come back in a few weeks now that I know what to expect and can prepare for it."

"Cal. Its a long way drive. We're here now. The details are fresh in our minds. Its going down tonight."

She threw her hands in the air and shook her head. "Fine! All because you want to save a few bucks! Well I got news for you mister... you are not going to do this alone!"

"What do you mean?"

"We're going to tag team this reading. I will be monitoring you remotely!"

"You mean, like the apartment?"

"Yes."

"What about Rudy?"

"As long as I'm in the trailer, he won't even notice. He'll think I'm meditating."

"All right then. Its settled. Let's get started."

"I still think this is a big mistake."

Josh blessed his brother marking a cross on Braden's forehead. "You sure about this?"

"I'll be fine, Dude. All I have to do is pay attention and take notes. I'll be in and out before you know it." He glanced at Caleigh. "Any last minute instructions?"

"Concentrate on the house's past. If you're able to retract time, the house itself will reveal the truth. The past is what it is."

"Okay. Anything else?"

"If at all possible, do not interact with the entity. It is deceitful and of no use to us. Observe from a distance and do your best to stay undetected. If it finds you, get out of there."

"Okee Doke."

## The Blessing

With a smile and flashlight in hand, Braden left his team and the Rentzells safe in the confines of the team trailer. Marching across the yard, his brave front gave way to doubt. *God, I hope I can do this.* He stepped on the porch. A chilly breeze brushed across his face. He took a look around and laughed it off. *Nice try.*

Once inside, he ascended the grand staircase. He peeked through the banister railing with each step. *Why does this remind me of The Ghost and Mr. Chicken?* He made it to the top with a loud creak from the top step. He quickly lifted his foot and stepped over the noisy board easing his way down the hallway.

Caleigh's warning rang in his ears. Braden approached the most active room in the house and peered through the doorway. *Let's get this over with.* Trying to shake his nerves, he entered and waved at the surveillance camera with a reassuring thumbs up.

His heart pounded hard in his chest. The slightest sound would have caused him jumping out of his skin. His head was on a swivel. His eyes jetted across the room like a gun turret. The ominous pentagram stared back at him with a threat. Taking a seat, he turned his back on its forbidding presence and assumed a cross-legged meditation position before reluctantly closing his eyes.

The first few minutes were agonizing. Unable to concentrate, having an unnerving sense of being watched, Braden coaxed the eyes in the back of his head to remain open. He reminded himself of surveillance to counteract the sensation. *Everyone is watching. Stop being a pus and man up.*

Drawing a deep breath provided a euphoric release and allowed him to let his inhibitions fade with each exhale. His physical existence no longer acknowledged his immediate surroundings. He began to drift slipping further into subconscious. Braden was on his way.

CHAPTER THIRTY ONE

# THE FAMILY THAT PRAYS TOGETHER

The sun was setting on a warm summer evening. A dirt road appeared under his feet. Off in the distance, the silhouette of a tall grain bin materialized in the purple and orange hues of day's end. Assuming the detail must mean something, he took the sign as a point of direction. The road's unnerving isolation formed under each step, fading into darkness as he passed. Its gravel crackled below his feet as he drudged on. He focused on the looming structure ahead. The bin's shadow cast an ominous vestige across the road resembling a gate of no return. Braden ignored its symbolic warning. His quest coaxed him forward.

The formidable cries of a dog yelping pierced the desolate silence. Its pleas for help convinced him to rush towards the commotion. The canine's desperation echoed from every direction until they came to an abrupt halt. His heart sank. He could only think that something awful had just happened.

Braden's intuition took over guiding him to a familiar driveway. He followed its path, and the Himmelberg farmhouse came into view. *Well, I made it.* Dusk surrendered to night allowing him to creep up on the Victorian under the cover of darkness. *Cal told me to stay in the shadows. I'll just peek through the window.*

The lights were out, but signs of life reverberated from within. An indiscernible conversation broke out coaxing him to peer through the window. No one was in sight. He slid along the wall to the next opening. *No one is in the study.*

Suddenly, a wavering glow appeared through the living room's stain glass. Chanting resonated through the walls and begged Braden to take a look. The distorted panes made details impossible leaving him at a disadvantage. Frustration gave way to carelessness, *I have to get inside. I've got to know.*

Caleigh's voice filled his head, *"Be careful. You don't want to be discovered!"*

Caleigh's admonitory puzzled Braden, *"I thought this was a residual vision?*

*"If any member of the house is sensitive,"* Caleigh advised, *"they will sense your presence. Keep your distance."*

He was skeptical of Caleigh's advice. His obstinance overrode her psychic theory. Without a second thought, Braden slipped in the back door. Once inside, he detected a strange scent. Sneaking through the study, he peeked around the door leading into the living room. Four heavily cloaked individuals faced the stain glass reciting a prayer. Under the window, an ornate wooden altar held four large red candles which bathed the room in an eerie glow. A wide gold canister emitted smoke responsible for the repulsive odor.

The scene was archaic yet captivating. It enticed him closer to the action. He was almost standing amongst the odd religious sect before realization struck him. He made a mental record of words the group repeated over and over again. *Blut ...Tier ...Damon ...opfern.* He peeked over one of the members shoulders and spotted something of great significance. There on the altar under the wide gold canister was a Ouija Board! *That has to be the same one! Same markings and everything. And there's the planchette.*

Caleigh popped in, *"Okay. Get out of there. That's enough!"*

Braden considered wrapping it up when the surreal service took a page out of the Aleister Crowley playbook. A fifth member carried in a dog with a gashing head wound. At first Braden thought the canine was dead. That is until he saw one of its legs twitching. Unable to interfere, Braden watched helplessly. The fifth member laid the animal on the makeshift altar. The animal flailed back and forth while the individual forcefully held it down.

The cloaked figure raised a ceremonial blade in the air and recited a few words. The other members waited in silence. He held down the dog's head plunging the knife deep into its neck. The act caused every nerve in the canine's body to stiffen one last time in its final struggle before it went completely limp.

Each member individually approached the altar and dipped a finger into the animal's fatal wound. Gazing upon the stain glass window, the worshippers uttered something in reverence before tracing a bloody line across their forehead.

*"Are you watching this, Cal?"*

Silence.

Braden repeated himself more persistently, *"Cal? Did you see that?"*

Again, no response.

The grotesque service came to a close. The cloaked figures began to remove their heavy robes. *Let's see who's who.*

A heavy set, middle aged male sporting a thin dark beard lining his jaw was responsible for the animal sacrifice. His thick eyebrows almost met in the middle, and a scar ran down his once broken nose. Obviously the leader, he instructed two younger males to remove the carcass while he extinguished the candles on the altar. Grabbing the wide gold canister and Ouija Board, he bowed then brought the items into the study. He placed both on his desk. The elder checked to see if anyone was looking. Once sure he was alone, he tucked the planchette behind a book on the top shelf lining the study's wall. *This just gets better by the minute.*

## The Blessing

Braden followed the old man back into the living room where he was met by a beautiful young lady. As she turned to speak, her protruding midsection exposed an up and coming birth.

Upset, she announced, "I saw the doctor today. He did an ultrasound. Its a girl."

The old man was not happy, "You know what to do."

She was on the verge of hysterics, "I won't! I won't do it!"

An angry scowl spread across his face, "Its a waste of time. I won't have it!"

The elder then pointed at the stain glass window, "He won't have it!"

The young lady dropped to her knees pleading, "Father! Please don't make me do this!"

The man slapped his begging daughter, "You promised me a son! Your brother is dead! I need a male descendant! Get rid of this abomination! Immediately!"

"Its not an abomination! Its our daughter!" the girl screamed. Getting to her feet in defiance, "I'm having this baby! If you won't have her, then someone else will!"

The young woman ran out of the room leaving her father silently staring at the stain glass window.

The staunch realization was all too clear to Braden. *My God, Mickie is the illegitimate daughter of her Grandfather? How can I tell her that?*

"You won't," the old man said out loud.

Braden assumed the old man was referring to his daughter's final outburst. He thought nothing of it and prepared for his return to the team.

The old man stood admiring the stained glass. Without turning his head, he said, "Where are you going?"

Braden paused, *Is he talking to me?*

"Who else would I be talking to?" the elder acknowledged.

*Can he see me?*

"No, but I know you're there."

Braden's cover was blown. Discretion turned to panic. He tried to make a break for it. A strange tingling sensation stung his lower extremities halting his exit. *What the fuck is this?* The floorboards of the study mysteriously engulfed his feet like quicksand rendering him shackled to the floor. The old man laughed as Braden fought to get free.

He called out, *"Caleigh! Caleigh, can you hear me!"*

The pleas went unanswered to the delight of the elder. His maniacal taunts coincided with the floorboards' appetite. They pulled Braden deeper into the wood grain. Up to his knees, Braden screamed louder, *"For the love of God, someone help me!"*

The room shook violently. The house itself was alive and moaning. It yanked the investigator down into its bowels devoured to his waist. Braden's leverage could no longer compete with the unforeseen power. The old man raised his arms in jubilation crying out, "Now, You are His!"

.

# BRIAN KENT

CHAPTER THIRTY TWO

# THE WAIT IS OVER

Helpless and abandoned, Braden's will to survive faded quickly. The torturous thought of being imprisoned in this nightmare sank deep into his soul. He could feel himself slipping into darkness when he heard a voice, "*Take my hand.*"

"*Cal?*"

"*Braden… take my hand.*"

A bright light gradually emerged from the study's hellbound shadows. From its glow, a hand extended. Knowing anything was better than his current predicament, Braden reached out in a leap of faith. A gentle tug released him from his treacherous bondage. The luminescence enveloped the investigator and cradled him like a small child. It channeled him far away from the agonizing ordeal. The warm bathing incandescence numbed his senses and relieved his pain and anguish.

"*Thanks, Cal. For a minute there, I thought I was a goner.*"

The celestial advocate remained anonymous, *"You are here now."*

*"Good. Glad to hear it. I have so much to report."*

There was no reply.

Braden was dumbfounded by the silent treatment and undefinable whereabouts. His patience wore thin. *"Come on, Cal. Let's get home."*

A whisper announced, *"You are home. I've been waiting for you."*

The statement left Braden questioning his ally's intentions. He remembered the synonymous position at the Dempster house. The thought of a similar confrontation systematically rose his defenses. He tried to conceal his lack of trust by wittingly expressing his desire to return to the team. *"Well, I haven't been gone that long, but I do need to get back!"*

*"How quickly, you forget,"* the voice replied.

Braden felt at a complete disadvantage. The unidentifiable surroundings offered no direction. Even if he could escape, the lack of focal point disturbed the investigator. The suspended animation brought comfort, yet it resembled a womb-like subjection. He feared he had traded one prison for another. He could feel his anxiety superseded appreciation, *"Whoever you are, this isn't funny anymore. Let me go!"*

A gentle kiss touched Braden's lips. *"But, you have my heart."*

## The Blessing

The words echoed through his mind taking him back to a certain kiss on the streets of the Old Market. *"Connie?"*

Braden's visual senses returned. A familiar pair of blue eyes emerged from the radiant nothingness. The form drew closer to embrace him. Their energy's meshed in a euphoric collision emulating the passionate love they once made. Over and over their entwined consciousness ravaged each other simulating every possible emotion between the two.

All care and concern went to the way side, *I was sure I'd never see you again!"*

*"I was always by your side."*

The past tense reference opened his eyes to a different reality putting the reunion on unwanted pause, *"Wait a minute. If I'm here with you, something must have happened."*

Connie expected the reaction, *"Yes, my love. Its your time."*

Braden shook his head not ready to grasp the final resolution. *"I have things to do. I have to get back. My Brother… the team!"*

*"I'm sorry, Dear. This was meant to be. This is your destination."*

*"Can I at least let Josh know I'm okay?"*

Connie stroked his cheek. She could feel his heart breaking. *"All in good time, my love. All in good time."*

BRIAN KENT

# CHAPTER THIRTY THREE

# A SECRET UNCOVERED

Sheriff Steinkamp's squad car pulled in shortly after the ambulance's arrival. The array of flashing lights saturated the Himmelberg's yard in red and blue. The lawman approached and recognized Elsa from their earlier meeting. He watched her rocking back and forth on the front porch. An emotional wreck, she did her best to keep her sobs to a minimum. He knew he had to handle the situation delicately. "Hello again, Ma'am. I assume you knew the deceased. I'm so sorry for your loss."

She blew her nose and wiped her swollen eyes. "Thank you."

"If you don't mind, I need to ask a few questions."

Elsa sat up straight. "All right."

"Thank you." The sheriff pulled out a pad and pen. "Can I get your take on this evening?"

Elsa cleared her throat. "Well... Braden went in to do a reading. He was only up there a few minutes when he went into convulsions. We thought it was part of the reading, so we left him alone. A few minutes later, he was lying motionless on the floor."

The officer squinted. "Okay, let me get this straight. Your friend was having a seizure, and no one helped?"

Elsa lifted her head with tears welling. "No! He was doing a reading. He's a psychic."

"Okay. I know what a psychic is. What's a reading?"

About that time, Caleigh made her way out the front door. She gave a sad smile. "Its okay, Elsa. I got this." She extended a hand to the officer. "Caleigh Brooks. I'm the team's psychic."

Steinkamp gave a firm grip before asking, "Okay, Miss Brooks, what's a reading?"

"Its a sensitive's meditative state of mind using the blessing God gave us to communicate with the other side."

The sheriff scribbled on his pad. "And is this a dangerous practice? Can this physically harm the individual attempting it?"

"Not fatally. At most, it can give you a headache or make you sick to your stomach. Nothing like this. I've been doing it for years and have never been seriously harmed."

"So how do you explain tonight's events?"

Cal let out a long sigh. "Braden had a heart attack a few weeks back. He wasn't taking very good care of himself. My guess is that something startled him during his session, and it triggered another coronary."

"Alright." He paused to collect his thoughts. "Elsa told me, you were watching this happen. Were some of you in there with him?"

"No. He was alone. We were monitoring him on surveillance."

"Were you recording this surveillance? If so, I'd like to see it."

"Yes, we were." Caleigh pointed at the trailer. "Our tech adviser, Rudy, is in there. He can help you."

The sheriff tipped his cap and then made his way to the team's portable base station. In the meantime, Daris and Garrett helped the EMT's carry the stretcher down from the second floor. Josh refused to let them cover his brother's face. Once outside, they lowered the wheels of the gurney. Josh had a hard time accepting the inevitable. The sight of the open doors on the ambulance shook denial into reality. It was more than he could take. "Come on, B... Fight dammit! You beat this before... You can do it!" He turned to the the EMT's. "Hit him again! I know he's in there somewhere!"

One of the medics replied, "He's gone, Mr. Cabrera. We've done everything we can. I'm so sorry."

Josh slammed his fist on Braden's chest, "Don't you do this to me, brother! This shit isn't funny anymore!"

Garrett stepped in and grabbed Josh by the shoulders. "He's gone, buddy. He's been gone half an hour."

Josh unwillingly let go of his brother's hand. He allowed the EMT's to pull the sheet over Braden's lifeless eyes. Garrett escorted Josh to the team trailer, where Sheriff Steinkamp offered his condolences. "So sorry for your loss, Mr. Cabrera."

Josh had nothing to say. Garrett addressed the lawman. "Did you get everything you need?"

The officer tucked his pad into his pocket. "Yeah, I think so. Your surveillance was a big help. It appears your friend simply had a heart attack. We'll know more after the autopsy."

Garrett nodded. "You've got our contact info. Keep us posted."

Once the sheriff and medical staff left the scene, a stillness fell over the farm. The team's grief rose to the surface with the escalating calls of a thousand crickets singing to the heart of the team's pain.

Daris and Garrett kept a distant but attentive eye on Josh who was sitting in the SUV's driver seat. Elsa still sat on the front porch staring at the sky. She seemed to be searching for a purpose behind her friend's demise. Rudy managed to sidestep his emotions. He found temporary solace in the surveillance monitor. Caleigh was left to deal with the shocked farm owners. Nodding with obligatory concern, her last debate with Braden drowned out the couple's verbal anxiety. She considered the intuition a call to action.

Still on the job, Cal called a team meeting with the Rentzells. Everyone loathed the idea, but they all grudgingly gathered on the front porch anyway. The psychic knew she had to gently navigate the river of emotion. "This loss is devastating. Our dear friend and leader will truly be missed. But I think all of you should know Braden's sacrifice was not in vain."

Daris piped up, "Oh yeah? How's that?"

"I was with Braden during his reading."

"Weren't you taking a nap?" Garrett asked.

"I was in meditation. I was remotely viewing his session."

Josh was not in the mood. "Do I want to hear this right now?"

An awkward silence fell upon the group. Elsa remarked, "Maybe its not a good time to discuss this."

Garrett added, "He just lost his brother for God's sake."

Caleigh thought otherwise. "He was the leader of this team... A brother to us all! He did this reading against my better judgment. This tells me he was prepared to do anything. He should be commended for that. If you want to respect his wishes, you need to hear me out."

Cal's chiding hit home leaving everyone speechless yet conflicted. She stood with head held high and waited.

Finally, Josh lifted his head and swiped away a tear. "She's right. He would want us to finish what we've started."

Until now, the Rentzell's took the team's reaction from a distance. However, the thought of continuing the night's investigation was a little more than they could take. Mickie spoke up, "Look... you guys don't have to do this. Our suspicions have been confirmed, and we are grateful. Its a relief to know we're not crazy. We didn't expect this much."

"But there's more," Caleigh uttered.

"Based on what?" Cory butted in. "Some hocus pocus bullshit?"

Caleigh flew off the handle. She turned a steely gaze on him. "That hocus pocus bullshit managed to take someone's life tonight! You better hear what I have to say before you end up in the same position!"

The tone struck a chord with the homeowner. He backpedaled to his corner, but the psychic wasn't finished. "I'm going to prove to you Braden's reading is accurate. Mr. Rentzell, go into the study and check the top shelf of your book case. There is something there relevant to your case."

Perplexed by the odd request and no longer prepared to dispute the psychic Cory agreed to the task. All the lights were on in the house. Its cozy appearance felt deceiving as Cory crossed his home's threshold. Caleigh's warning shifted his imagination into overdrive. He flinched with each creak of the floor. Clenching his fists, he prepared himself to take a swing at anything that moved. Cautiously he tip toed into the study. His eyes targeted the top ledge of the bookcase. *I don't see anything. Maybe its small.* He ran his hand across the highest plank. One of his fingers brushed a wooden object tucked in the corner.

He managed to nab it and pulled it down along with years of dust. *Huh? What an odd thing to leave up there.*

Surprised by the discovery, Cory quickly emerged from the house to rejoin the others. "All I found was this piece of wood. Kinda looks like a table for a doll house."

The item brought Josh to his feet at full attention. "Is that what I think it is? How did you know?"

"Yes, its the planchette." Caleigh said evenly. "Braden saw Mickie's father place it there."

Mickie interrupted. "Braden saw my father?"

Cal's hand encompassed Mickie's. "And your mother."

Mickie was beside herself. "Please tell me everything. I want to know."

The psychic knew the truth was going to hit below the belt. She sighed deeply. "Sometimes its best to leave the past in the past."

"So... Its bad, isn't it?"

"Your family left you a beautiful home, and your mother loved you very much. It was her decision alone, to bring you into this world. It was her decision to spare you from your family's past."

"Then why leave me this house? We already know there is something wrong with it! Now we're stuck!"

"She's right, Cal," Josh added. "They have a right to know."

Reluctantly, Cal recounted the events of the reading. "Braden found himself on this property shortly before you were born. At that time, I'm assuming your Grandparents owned it. During the reading, he walked in on a cult-like ceremony being conducted in your living room. Judging by the cloaks being worn, the prayers recited, the inclusion of the Oujia Board, and an animal sacrifice, I would guess the service to be pagan, possibly satanic in nature."

Mickie gasped, "Oh dear God!"

The latest development drew Elsa's interest. "So those animal carcasses on the road could have been from here."

"More than likely." Caleigh continued, "After the ceremony, Braden remained in the study where he saw your Grandfather place the planchette on the top shelf. That's how I knew where it was."

Cory nodded his head.

"And now, the unpleasant part." The psychic shook her head dreading the detail. "Braden overheard a conversation between your grandfather and your mother. He was demanding a termination of a pregnancy. Your birth."

A lump rose in Mickie's throat. "He didn't want me?"

"It wasn't that he didn't want you, sweet pea. He wanted a male heir."

Mickie looked at her confused. "For what? The farm?"

"Possibly. That among other things."

"Am I to assume I'm an only child? Where was my father in all of this?"

## The Blessing

Caleigh knew the truth was going to shake her client to the core. She bent forward, looked deep into Mickie's eyes, and gently took her hands. "My dear... your grandfather is your father."

Not one mouth was closed. Mickie tried to process the horrific news. She scrambled into her husband's arms crying. The devastating announcement left everyone except Garrett inarticulate. "Well that certainly explains the adoption."

Caleigh changed the subject. "We already know the house is active. I believe the rituals are responsible."

Cory, who was still comforting his wife, looked up at Cal. "Meaning?"

"A house cleansing and blessing," the psychic advised. "Worst case scenario, an exorcism."

A loud crash echoed from inside causing everyone to jump. Rudy flew out of the trailer. "You're not going to believe this shit! Something just knocked that statue over in the master bedroom!"

# BRIAN KENT

## CHAPTER THIRTYFOUR

# DOWN THE RABBIT HOLE

Caleigh's perception was no longer hogwash to the homeowners who were now contemplating a change in residency. Cory asked, "Is this going to work?"

Caleigh glanced at him. "I can't guarantee anything. I've never had to deal with an inanimate object of this scale."

Josh handed her a bundle of white sage. "What do mean by that?"

"We're not dealing with a lone spirit here. Its the house itself."

"I don't understand." Cory raised an eyebrow. "Are you saying the house is a ghost?"

"No. Your home is like a sponge. Its harboring everything the Himmelberg's have introduced and accepted within its walls." Caleigh, busy with the preparations, "The house has absorbed all of this energy, which has essentially given it a life of its own."

Josh squinted in disbelief. "Are you sure about this? I mean this sounds down the rabbit hole even by my standards."

Caleigh politely asked Cory for a minute alone. Once she had Josh to herself, she looked him squarely in the eyes with stern resolve. "I understand you are not capable of seeing what I see. I only ask you to trust me. With that being said," she paused to take a deep breath, "I want you to know your brother is alright."

"Were you there when he passed? What was the cause?"

"I'm assuming mental stress and anxiety set off a heart attack." She glanced down. "Unofficially... the house tried to consume him."

"What?"

"Pull up a chair. I need you to understand this." Once Josh took a seat, she continued, "Braden's reading filled in a lot of blanks. For at least two to three generations, the Himmelberg clan has been involved in questionable practices. Parts of your brother's vision and Elsa's research have confirmed that. These rituals were fairly common in old Germany and were more than likely brought over and continued here." She paused to evaluate how much he was taking in before continuing. "Now normally, these are simple pagan customs requesting a blessing on the land. However, as time went on, someone introduced animal sacrifice and the Ouija Board. These changes may have drawn in negative energy. This negativity convinced its worshipers to leave the board's spiritual door wide open. This is why the planchette and board were deliberately separated. God knows what came through, but its my guess the accumulative energy is now rooted within these walls."

Josh leaned back, his right leg bouncing nervously. "What did you mean by consume him?"

"Braden was so far removed from his physical presence that he was unaware his body was giving out. His heart actually stopped shortly before the end of his reading, yet I was able to consciously remain in contact. He had no idea he had passed, and the house took advantage of that. Your brother visualized the floorboards ingesting him when, in fact, it was the house attempting to absorb his consciousness. Physically, he didn't feel a thing."

Josh bowed his head, "Is he all right?"

"I believe he crossed. There at the end of the reading I could no longer hear or sense his energy. That usually indicates a surpassing of the final barrier."

The word final sucker punched the younger brother and shook reality's dismissed truth loose from his self-induced confines. He choked on an onslaught of tears and fought back the strangling sensation. It was just long enough for him to pray. "I know you can hear me... I know you'll be fine... Dear God... let me know he's okay... let me know he made it."

Both teammates broke out in a much needed outburst. They allowed the pent up heartache to explode upon each other's shoulder. The embrace alleviated the volcanic buildup of emotion. Josh rubbed his red swollen eyes. "Braden should've packed a bag. I'm sure its a long trip."

The liberating release led to a requisite of laughter. Josh chuckled before clearing his throat. "All right. We have a house full of unwanted guests with bad intentions. What's the game plan?"

"Mickie needs to lead the charge. The Himmelberg's started this. Its going to take a Himmelberg to finish it."

# CHAPTER THIRTY FIVE

# A CHANGE IN TACTICS

"**Y**ou sure you're up for this?" Daris asked the youngest brother while handing him equipment. "This is a pretty tall order."

Josh lifted his head and squared his shoulders. "I'm good." He narrowed his eyes slightly. "Got a score to settle."

Rudy, who stood nearby, addressed his fiance. "No meditation or readings, right? This is just a simple cleansing."

Caleigh didn't want to hear any more scolding. "One of our closest friends lost his life tonight. I'm going to do anything I can to rectify that. Just go to your monitor and keep an eye on things." Her voice had a cold edge to it. "Don't tell me how to do my job."

Elsa and Garrett assisted Mickie into a vest of equipment and gave her a brief explanation of their uses. "Leave this antenna fully extended." Garrett point to the item. "If it goes off, a stray EMF is close by."

"Is that a bad thing?"

Elsa laid a reassuring hand on her shoulder. "For now, let's just say an unaccounted energy source is in your proximity and leave it at that."

Cory stepped closer to his wife. Worry lines creased his face. "Is she going to be okay?"

Cal stepped in and placed a protective arm around Mickie. "She will be right by my side. None of us will be separated."

"Is there anything I can do?" Cory asked.

Elsa thought for a moment. "Do you have anything that can remove magic marker?"

"From what?"

"Once we cleanse your child's bedroom, we'll need that drawing removed from the floor," Cal explained without hesitation.

"I have a belt sander. Will that work?"

A smile spread across Cal's face. "Perfect. I'll let you know when to start."

Caleigh delegated the last minute instructions. "Okay, Rudy and Elsa on surveillance. Daris and Garrett, I want you two to go room to room and open every window, door, nook and cranny in front of us. Once we have completed a room, I need you to close everything up. Then sea salt the entrance to that space."

"Gotcha." All four answered in unison.

"After the house has been cleansed, we will finish by closing the Ouija and properly dispose of the board. Any questions?"

Everyone stood stalk still waiting for the signal to go.

Cal nodded. "Good. Let's get started."

Caleigh led Mickie and Josh through the front door where they were greeted by a stale, musty odor. It resembled that of a previously flooded house that had never been reopened. The air was humid immediately causing beads of sweat to appear on their foreheads. The stifling atmosphere became increasingly unbearable the further they advanced into the home. "Is the AC on?" Josh asked.

"Last time I checked it was still going," Mickie replied.

"Its the house," Caleigh advised. "It knows."

They reached the attic and commenced with prayer. Cal handed Mickie the bundle of white sage, which she lit. Mickie then fanned its smoke with an eagle feather throughout all four corners of the dark loft. Its cleansing scent overpowered the residual stench the house, seemingly emitted in protest.

Josh sprinkled the holy water around the outer edges of the room. The single light bulb overhead flickered as each drop fell to the ground. Josh ceased the dowsing for fear of losing the light. "Keep going!" Cal ordered with authority. "Don't let it deter you!"

The hundred year old structure stirred like a sleeping giant. Its aged support beams and floor joists moaned as if its slumber had been interrupted. All three meticulously went about their duties ignoring the objections. Caleigh took point on their charge. The psychic remained steadfast in her conviction. "Sancte Michael Archangele defende nos in proelio contra nequitiam et insidias diaboli esto praesidium, Imperat illi dues supplices depracumar tuque princeps militiae coelestis satanum aliosque spiritus malignos, qui ad perditionem animarum pervagantur in mundo divina virtute in infernum detrude. Amen"

Mickie pulled Josh aside. "Is she speaking German?"

"No. That's Latin. She's reciting St. Michael's prayer for protection."

Caleigh gave Daris and Garrett a nod to close the room. Both sensed vibrations in the floor. It sent a tingling sensation up their legs. The home's tantrum encouraged both to hastily dispense the salt across the attic's threshold almost spilling the entire bag in the process. "Easy, Guys." Caleigh commanded. "We have a lot of rooms to seal."

Suddenly, Caleigh was knocked to the floor. Her Latin prayer book flew out of her hand and down the back stairwell. Garrett helped her to her feet, "Jesus Christ, Cal! This is getting dangerous!"

Caleigh paid no heed to Garrett's apprehension. Instead she cried out to the walls around her, "Those of you who wish to leave... are free from your earthly chains! The door is open... Go and find your peace!"

The house let off an aftershock. All five lost their balance and staggering down to the next level. Mickie looked around wildly. "I don't want to do this anymore!"

*The Blessing*

Caleigh stepped in front of her and grabbed her by the shoulders. She stared  at her dead in the eye. "Do you want to give up? Are you relinquishing the house?"

Mickie sobbed on the cusp of hysterics. "I can't live like this!"

"Then don't," Cal said sternly. Her tone offered strength. "Take back your home. Its a physical object in a physical existence. You are part of that physical existence; they are not. You are stronger than they are." She gave Mickie's shoulders a firm squeeze as if to infuse her with determination and empowerment. "Do something about it!" she shouted.

Mickie screamed, "GET THE FUCK OUT OF MY HOUSE!"

A loud crash of glass breaking echoed up from the lower level. Everyone jumped simultaneously then froze in their tracks. After a long silence that seemed to drag on for an eternity, Josh called out, "What in the fuck?"

Rudy's voice came blaring over the walkie talkie, "Josh! The stain glass window in the living room literally exploded! There's glass everywhere! I'm on my way to check it out."

"Jesus," Josh muttered, pulling his walkie out in response, "Alright. I'll send Garrett down to help."

The latest uproar paused the cleansing and left the group in a huddle questioning their next move. Theory bounced back and forth in a flurry of opinion. Cal put an end to the debate. "Shhhhh…" She held a finger to her lips and glanced around. "Have any of you noticed how quiet it is?"

The eerie silence brought a false sense of security. Sighs of relief replaced the bedlam of dispute. Josh rubbed Mickie's shoulder. "See what happens when you push your weight around?"

"Are we done then?"

Cal wasn't buying it. "No. You don't understand. There is no sound at all."

"Meaning?" Mickie looked genuinely confused.

"I'm not sure. Without opening up, I'm third eye blind here. But I am certain…" She paused again. "This isn't right."

"Okay," Josh acknowledged. "Then we keep going. We are obviously making an impact."

"Most definitely." Caleigh added, "But keep your eyes open. I think its gearing up to change tactics."

They cautiously entered the master bedroom. Pieces of the St. Michael's statue crunched under their feet. Mickie kicked the fragments out from in front of her. "I didn't like that statue anyway."

Everyone but Caleigh seemed to feed off Mickie's new found confidence. Going room to room, they cleansed all but the child's bedroom on the second floor. The lack of resistance troubled Cal. About to enter the most volatile space in the house, she asked, "Daris? I want you to bring up the thermal imaging camera and the Ouija. Tell Cory to bring in the sander."

He handed Josh the bag of sea salt. "Will do."

*The Blessing*

Cal coached Mickie and Josh. "Okay. I don't want to frighten you, but this is far from over. It takes a lot of energy to destroy physical objects. Energy this strong doesn't just go away easily. Both of you need to go about your business, and ignore anything that may happen. And I do mean anything." She turned to the homeowner. "Mickie, I need you to follow my instructions to the letter. Understand?"

"Understood."

All three finished the room without a single interruption leaving Cal really on edge. *This can't be over. Where is it hiding?*

Daris returned. "Here's the board."

"Place it on the pentagram," Caleigh ordered. "Where's the planchette?"

"I thought you had it."

"No. It was on the desk sitting on top of the board in the trailer."

Daris sucked in his breath. "That makes two things missing. I can't find Cory either."

# BRIAN KENT

# CHAPTER THIRTY SIX

# CORY?

The house cleansing was at a stand still. With daybreak only two hours away, stress and fatigue brought an onslaught of yawning and red eyes. The respite left time for reflection on the evening's loss leading Josh to a bottle of Jack Daniels.

Caleigh refocused everyone's attention. "Every time we are interrupted, it allows this thing to regain strength. It is imperative to apply constant pressure in order to weaken its ability. Once we start the cleansing, we must remain consistent. Before we start again, we need that planchette and we need to find Cory."

Everyone went their separate ways while a worried Mickie checked out the old barn. Cory's pickup was still in the yard, but locked. *He wasn't in the house. He's got to be out here.* She called out, "Honey? You in there?"

The lack of response only amplified the dead calm which had fallen across her property. *No breeze… No crickets… Nothing.*

Every muscle in her body battled tension's paralyzing effect. She drudged further into the dilapidated structure. With each struggling step she stopped and peered into the foreboding darkness. Her intuition screamed a warning in her head, yet her desire to put an end to the madness pushed her forward. Engulfed in the barn's black interior, she whimpered, "Hello?... Cory?"

She searched the searing darkness, her pupils as wide as her retina's. The tall black outline of a man appeared at the opposite end of the barn. It stood motionless with arms at its side facing her in a defensive stance. Mickie was fairly certain it was her husband. "What are you doing out here? We need you inside."

The shadow replied, "I'm looking for the sander."

"Do you need help?"

The figure slid out of view without a single word.

"Maybe if you turn on a light you could see!"

Her suggestion was again greeted with dead silence.

Mickie waded through the barn's weed infested unused cattle stalls. She nearly fell flat on her face once or twice. "For God's sake, Cory, turn on a fucking light!"

Something hit her hard from behind. Mickie's head slammed into one of the stall's four by fours. She landed flat on her back in a daze. An obese old man hovered over her with his pants down around his ankles. He reeked of alcohol and body odor. A maniacal grin spread across his face. He reached for her waist and yanked her pants down. Then he positioned himself between her legs and knelt between her quivering thighs. Grabbing her by the arms, he pinned her to the floor. Drool dripped from his revolting smirk as he seductively whispered in her ear, "Mannlichen erben."

He forced himself inside her. Mickie struggled for a footing to buck him off. He used her tangled blouse to control her now flailing hands which were clawing at his face. She let out a shrilling scream, managing to get one of her arms free. She covered her face to block the pungent scent of his breath. In doing so, her swinging elbow connected against the side of his head, splitting his ear wide open.

He reared back in pain, letting go of her other arm. Shaking his head to regain composure, Mickie took the opportunity to make a break for it. But he grabbed for her wrist, pulled her closer, and slapped her across the face with such force, it nearly knocked Mickie unconscious.

Out of nowhere, Daris and Garrett charged the assailant. Using their shoulders, they bull rushed the rapist, sending him flying into the wall. Daris immediately jumped to his feet squaring up with both fists ready. The dazed old man struggled up the wall and to his feet. Daris didn't give him a chance to retaliate. He delivered a devastating right cross rendering the aggressor incapacitated. Garrett shined his flashlight in the attacker's face.

"CORY!?" Mickie yelped.

"Are you okay, Mick?" Garrett asked.

Mickie reached up to examine her head. She felt a solid lump on her forehead where she'd been hit. "I think so." She turned a mortified gaze to her husband who was out cold. "I'd like to know what the hell got into him!"

Caleigh came running. "Tell me what happened."

"I got shoved into that board and hit my head. The next thing I knew, an old man was trying to rape me. The pig whispered something in my ear. That's when those two knocked him off."

"What did he say?" Elsa inquired.

"I don't know... It was gibberish. Man-lee-kem Urban something."

"That's German for male heir."

Cory stirred in the overgrowth of weeds along the barn wall. He rubbed his jaw and used his other hand to prop himself up slightly. "What the fuck am I doing in here?... And why do I feel like I just got ran over by train?"

Garrett and Daris stood over him ready to take action if needed. "Easy dude. Just take it easy. We had a little problem."

"What do mean 'we had a little problem'? Where's my wife?"

"I'm right here. Right where you left me, you sonofabitch!"

Cal stepped in. "My dear, Cory is not to blame here. Your husband was under an influence. And a powerful one at that."

Cory was visibly upset. "What you mean under the influence? I haven't had anything to drink since noon!" he spat.

"Both of you stop, right now," Caleigh ordered. "That's not what I'm referring to." The psychic turned to Mickie. "When you were attacked, was it a middle aged man with a thin beard and bushy eyebrows?"

"Yes!" Mickie exclaimed. "And a scar running down his nose!"

"That sounds like your Grandfather."

Daris looked around at everyone a bit confused. "There was no old man in here? Garrett and I caught Cory on top of her."

"My guess is Mickie was knocked out for a minute or two. In her state of unconsciousness she witnessed a residual reconstruction of the day she was conceived."

Mickie sat opened mouthed for a moment looking puzzled. "So, are you insinuating my Mother was raped? How does Cory fit into all of this?"

"I believe your Grandfather was using Cory to carry out the act again. And yes. I do believe your Mother was raped... more than likely it was carried out right here in the barn."

Cory looked mortified at Daris. "I was raping my wife?"

"No. But you were on top of her holding her down. When we heard her scream, Garrett and I ran in and knocked you off. Sorry about that."

"No apology necessary," he said with wide eyes. He turned to his wife. His color three shades paler than normal. "I'm so sorry, honey. I can't remember any of it."

Caleigh added, "Its perfectly understandable. None of this is your fault."

"No! Really? Its not!?" Cory spouted. "None of this is understandable! I just tried to hurt my wife! This bastard needs to go down!"

Josh stepped in, his voice cold and determined, "And that's exactly what we intend to do."

Garrett and Daris helped Cory to his feet. He staggered and fell down hard on his butt. "Damn, what the hell did I fall on?" He reached into his back pocket, "Its this thing." He handed the planchette to Josh.

The avenging brother grasped it and gave Cory a slight nod. "Now, we finish this."

CHAPTER THIRTYSEVEN

# REDEMPTION

Back on surveillance, Rudy kept a watchful eye on the gathering in the child's bedroom. White candles filled the room accenting the billows of smoke from the burning white sage. The house was completely cleansed, blessed, and sealed. The Ouija and pentagram closings were all that was left to finish. Every meter and detector available were strategically placed. Daris observed on thermal imaging, and Garrett recorded on a full spectrum camera. The room was covered, and every precaution was taken.

Caleigh placed the Ouija Board in the center of the pentagram, "Elsa? Josh? We need you to join us. The more participants, the better."

Reluctantly agreeing, both joined Mickie, Cory, and Caleigh on the floor. Each gently placed a finger on the planchette centered on the board. Caleigh instructed, "We are not interested in contact. Do not ask questions. If the board tries to communicate, remove your finger. Understood?"

With everyone in agreement, Caleigh began, "We are opening this door for the very last time. Those of you who no longer wish to remain may go now. We are allowing you safe passage along with our hopes and prayers. May you find peace in the light."

The planchette stirred for a moment, then stopped. Caleigh's encouragement continued, "We are freeing you from your earthly bondage. You have nothing to fear. Love and light await you on the other side. Go with our blessings."

The wooden piece remained still.

"Um, Cal?" Daris interrupted. "Not sure if this is one of our guests, but thermal is picking up a dark blue figure on your left."

"Is it moving?" Josh asked. "What's it look like?"

"It just seems to be hovering over Cal."

Josh asked the psychic, "You feeling anything?"

"Not really. I'm completely shut down, and I don't dare open up right now. Not in the middle of this." She instructed Daris, "Keep an eye on it."

The distraction managed to deter everyone's attention from the board. No one noticed the planchette intentionally move over the word, No. Unaware of its voluntary placement, Caleigh slid the piece to the middle of the board ready to start again, "Okay everyone."

Independently, the planchette lurched from under her finger. It slid directly over the negative response. Josh jumped back stuttering, "Whoa, whoa whoa...we got company!"

## The Blessing

Caleigh called out, "We are not here to communicate. This door will be closed permanently. This is your last chance. If you wish to leave... LEAVE NOW!"

The psychic tried to slide the piece into the starting position, but it wouldn't budge. The planchette stuck to the board refusing to be physically manipulated.

"I've had enough of your shit, Himmelberg! Let go of the piece!"

The wooden piece violently leapt from her fingers, slammed against the wall, and ricocheted into one of the candles knocking it the floor. Garrett immediately grabbed the piece and handed it back to the psychic. Then he placed the candle back into position.

"Is any of this being picked up on full spectrum or thermal?" Josh shouted.

"I still have it on thermal," Daris responded moving around the circle. "It appears to be pacing."

"You guys all right?" Rudy called out over the radio. "I'm picking up an anomaly on surveillance... like a transparent disturbance!"

"We're okay!" Josh responded. "Let us know of any changes!"

The Rentzell's sat in shock over the latest development. Cory couldn't dispute what his eyes had just witnessed. "This is fucking crazy!" He stood up and grabbed his wife's hand. "I say we move out. Tonight!"

Mickie was pissed, "No! I refuse to let him win!"

Cal echoed her sentiment, "That's it, girl! We need to finish this, and you are the one who's going to do it!"

Caleigh firmly placed the planchette on the board's starting point, "Everyone get in here... keep your finger pressed down on the piece!"

All five followed her instruction. "Now, Mickie... take back your home! Remove your Father from the premises!"

No longer afraid, the homeowner's adrenalin sent waves of angst through her body shaking as she cried out, "Look, you sonofabitch... this is my family's property! You are disgrace to the Himmelberg name! You are a disgusting stain on our heritage! I am a Himmelberg... This is my house now! I am turning my back on you... like you turned your back on me, you fucking revolting piece of shit! You wanted a deal with the devil... I hope you rot in hell! GET THE FUCK OFF OF MY PROPERTY!"

The planchette gradually began to move in a figure eight under their fingertips picking up speed with each pass. Caleigh shouted, "The door is unlocked! Those of you who have been kept here... now is your chance to leave! Go now with our blessings!"

A cool yet gentle breeze drifted through the room. The flames on each candle pointed the way. The sage's plumes followed a unified direction.

Cory looked around bewildered. "What's happening?"

## The Blessing

Caleigh could only think of one word, "Redemption."

Faint sounds of rejoice and laughter could be heard in the cleansing zephyr passing by the participant's heads. The sage's residual scent gradually cleared the air. The commotion went on for what seemed like an eternity leaving everyone in a state of awe and wonder. Garrett and Daris panned their cameras around the room, afraid they might miss something. Though startling, the flurry of activity was peaceful, casting a calm over its witnesses.

The planchette gracefully slowed its vigorous motion, similar to a turnstile completing a crowd's release. A simultaneous sigh of relief was expelled. Caleigh asked Daris, "Is our guest gone?"

Daris scanned the room one last time, "I think... we are clear."

"Good." The psychic addressed Mickie, "Place both of your hands on the piece, announce your name, who you are, verbally disclose your intent to close your family's board, and then slide the piece over the word goodbye."

Mickie cleared her throat nervously. She followed the instructions to the letter, "My name is Mickayla Himmelberg-Rentzell. I am a Himmelberg. I own this property and this house. I am officially closing this board forever!"

Once the planchette was slid into its final position, the group erupted in a emancipating outburst of cheers and applause. Cory's cynical smirk was replaced by a genuine smile. He fervently thanked each member of the team.

Mickie handed Caleigh the board. "Please get rid of this so no one will ever use it again."

"Consider it done."

CHAPTER THIRTY EIGHT

# YOU'VE GOT MAIL

Josh sat in his car waiting on the tow truck's arrival. The empty parking lot left plenty of room for the driver to hook up his brother's Explorer. The memorial service was still fresh in his mind. He laid Braden's urn on his lap. He affectionately ran his fingers across the gold embossed name on top. The date of death looked back at him with a resounding finality. *No more golf. No more football games. No more late night's at the race track. No more concerts.* A rap on the car window interrupted the tender recollections. He rolled down the window.

The greasy mechanic flicked a cigarette, "You, Josh Cabrera?"

"Yes." Josh pointed, "That's the SUV. When you get to my house, leave it in the street."

Dreading the task at hand, Josh was conflicted over Braden's belongings. The inevitable conclusion was forcing the youngest brother to split the items amongst close friends and teammates. The burden of division was his and his alone.

Slipping the key into the knob, he entered the loft which hadn't been occupied in over a month. It was hot, stale, and musty. The locked in scent of residual cigarette smoke, fast food leftovers, and alcohol wafted through the doorway. The time capsule was just as Braden left it.

Josh slid open the patio door and stepped out onto the small terrace overlooking Farnam Street. The city was alive with bar hops, live music bleeding into the streets, and the lone sound of police siren in the distance. The city's cold, careless reality reminded him how insignificant his loss was to the world. *Life goes on.* He turned to go back inside when a small bottle of Fireball laying on the deck table caught his eye. Twisting the cap off, he raised the shooter to the sky, "Did you leave this one for me?"

He had three weeks to get the apartment cleaned out but was in no hurry to erase this part of Braden's life. Josh took his time emptying ash trays, picking up trash, and even washing the few dishes left in the sink. Cleaning up somehow made it look as if Braden was expecting company. He broke the solitude by cranking up one of his brother's Kix CD's. The thunderous guitar and drums took him back to one of their notorious Fat Jak's after hour parties, briefly dashing his solemn mood.

Nodding to the beat, Josh meandered down the hallway to the master bedroom. The unmade bed brought his brother's philosophy to mind, *'Why make it if you're just going to mess it up later'.* He left it in its pristine condition. On the nightstand next to an empty bottle of Jack Daniels stood the little ghost figurine Connie had given his brother. *I wonder if...* he swallowed hard, *they found each other?*

He wandered into the bathroom and turned on the light. The broken mirror reminded him of Braden's exodus and change of address. *I wonder if Camfield is still around.* Josh carefully swept up the shards. Then he removed the remaining glass in the mirror's framework. *Old man Callahan ain't going to like this.*

The mental bombardment of Braden's world became overwhelming. It was too soon. The loft itself spewed an onslaught of memories. Everything screamed his brother's name. He took a break in the living room to clear his head. He struggled with the painful separation and his attempt to refocus. He entertained a different idea, *What if I take over the apartment? The rent is comparable. I could break my lease, move in a few things, and sell the rest.* The thought offered an island of solace in his ocean of anguish. *It could be like a living memorial.*

The sentiment brought on a sudden urge for a drink. *He has to have a stash in here somewhere.* Josh went through the cupboards digging behind boxes of oatmeal, bags of potato chips, and canned soup. *He was always good at hiding things.* He went through the closets and Braden's dresser drawers. The frantic search led him to the pantry. He ran his hand along the shelves above the washer and dryer. He pulled down a large box of laundry detergent.

Something rattled inside.  He pulled out a fifth of vodka. "Thank you, Brother!"

Making himself a screwdriver with outdated orange juice, he sat at the dining room table gazing out over the sun setting on the Omaha skyline. He finished his drink and went straight from the bottle. The alcohol served its purpose, numbing his senses. He staggered to his feet, "Why the fuck did you have to be so stubborn? You just had to go in there, didn't ya!? Well... you really did it this time!"

Josh's cell phone began to ring. He dug it out of his pocket and answered. Only static greeted him from the other end. "Hello?... This is Josh."

Still no reply. He hung up and placed the phone down on the table. It rang again.

The caller ID showed unknown caller. He answered, "Hello. Who is this?"

This time the deafening static caused Josh to pull the phone from his ear. He put it on speaker. Through the hissing white noise, one word crackled, "Josh!"

"This is Josh! You're breaking up... I can hardly hear you!"

The call ended abruptly with a loud click leaving the youngest brother wondering if someone was in trouble. Without a number, he hit redial. No one answered the return call. *Oh well... if they need me, they'll call again.*

Suddenly, a faint blue light emitted down the hall. A little uneasy, his adrenalin superseded his drunken stupor. *Is this the kind of shit he was dealing with? This better not be Camfield?*

Josh crept down the hallway to find the source emanating from Braden's office. He peeked around the door jam. His brother's laptop appeared to be in operation. Making his way behind the desk, a screen saving photo of the two brothers stared back at him. Josh took a seat at the desk. His shoulders slumped under the weight of his grief. "We had some great times. I hope you're all right."

A beep of notification pierced the silence, popping a number one over the computer's desktop mailbox. *Hmm... maybe its the person who tried to call.*

Clicking on it, Braden's email listing shot across the screen. Pulling up the most recent entry, the message was a simple, "Ok"

*Hmm... Who sent this?*

The bottle fell from Josh's hand. The sender read, BCabrera.com.

# BRIAN KENT

## ABOUT THE AUTHOR

Brian Kent is the founder and lead investigator of Paracon Investigations, a paranormal organization in Eastern Nebraska. The team has conducted well over three hundred investigations since its inception in 2007, making it one of the most experienced teams in the country.

Kent uses actual cases and experiences as a guideline in his fictional accounts leaving the line between reality and fantasy blurred. He believes the lessons learned on these cases will benefit those who struggle with similar circumstances. Its his intention to push the reader towards a better understanding of this phenomena and level of existence.

Kent has penned three non-fiction books including: *The House on Lincoln Street*, *Exploring Conscious Energy*, and *The Paracon Investigations 2007-2014*. His first fiction work, *The Reveal*, is the predecessor to *The Blessing* which is the second in the series.

BRIAN KENT

# ACKNOWLEDGEMENTS

*A special thanks to my writing team;*

*Editor - Marinda Dennis*
*Cover Art - Alicia Mattern*
*Format - Lisa Kovanda*

Also to my Paracon Investigations team, and
you, my readers. You make it worthwhile.

# BRIAN KENT

*The Blessing*

Made in the USA
Columbia, SC
15 January 2022